THE
FORGOTTEN

CLINT WESTGARD

ALSO BY CLINT WESTGARD

The Shadow Men:

    Realm of Shadows

    Council of Shadows

    Dance of Shadows

The Sojourners Cycle:

    The Forgotten

    The Apostate

    The Acolyte (forthcoming)

    The Double (forthcoming)

    The Sojourner (forthcoming)

The Maleficio Chronicles

The Devious Kind (a mystery)

Published by Lost Quarter Books
www.lostquarterbooks.com

This edition 2016

Cover image: © Agsandrew | Dreamstime.com

ISBN: 978-1-928035-19-0

For Mary Shelley

CONTENTS

ONE:

THE SEEKER

1

I remember nothing but this moment right now, as I walk through this park alone. Before, there was only darkness— not even darkness, something without substance at all. I emerged, whole but flailing, my feet carrying me forward before any thought or awareness had taken form. It is as though all that had been left behind, scraped away, in my journey from the void to this place.

The park is the sort one can find in any city, with grass and trees, footpaths winding their way through the greenery, and benches set at intervals upon which people sit. The surrounding neighborhood is equally unremarkable, a mixture of houses and apartment buildings with not a landmark among them. There is what looks like a school at the park's far end, with a yard fenced off from the rest of the park and turned into soccer and baseball fields.

I have no memories. How did I come to be here? Clearly I was walking from somewhere, with some destination in mind. These facts elude me.

My perception seems heightened, my senses keen to the slightest shifts in shadow and light, a breeze the cause of astonishment. It is as though I have been denied these basic sensations for so long that a minuscule change appears momentous. A cacophony of sound reaches my ears: the symphony of leaves rustling, the hum of cars on pavement, and the indecipherable murmurs of people around me. As they pass by I am entranced by their expressions, fleeting emotions slipping across their face that it seems only I am aware of.

Ahead of me a dog barks, quick and sharp, cutting through the clatter of sound and drawing my focus. It is led by a couple, perhaps in their early fifties. I follow them as they go along the path, listening to their conversation, though it is in a language I do not recognize. He appears to be Japanese, though I am certain that is not the language he is speaking. This seems significant to me and I listen to each intonation the couple makes, certain somehow that if I can unravel this code I can understand what is happening.

No meaning comes to me, and when they turn to the left to continue on the path around the park, I keep going straight, heading down the nearest street. At the next corner I turn right, my legs seeming to remember what my mind cannot. I trust them, going where instinct leads me, trying to empty my mind of any thought. Eventually I come to an apartment building, five or six stories tall, white and sickly green colors marking its exterior. I stand uneasily by the door until I fish in my jacket pocket and find a set of keys, one of which works, so I let myself in.

The air in the lobby is very warm, as if someone had left the heat on, even though it feels like summer. There is an odd, malingering odor; old carpets and humidity, I think. The lobby is filled with fake plants and battered furniture, remnants of a previous age. There is a mailroom to my left and a man steps out from it, a clutch of fliers in his hand, startling me. He seems not to notice my surprise, giving me the briefest of glances and a nod. Has he recognized me, or is he simply being polite?

I follow him upstairs, automatically continuing on to

the third floor as he steps off at the second, and find myself before room 304. I try my keys, knocking on the door as I unlock it, and enter.

"Hello," I call out tentatively, the sound of my voice shocking me.

I ignore that for the moment, ignore the creeping sense of terror I feel at all the blank spaces around my thoughts. Instead I explore the apartment, trying desperately to find something I recognize and can cling to in this storm of the unfamiliar. I go from the kitchen to the living room to the bedroom, opening closets and drawers. There are several bookshelves and I study their contents, as well as the CDs and movies spread out on the floor by the television and stereo. None of it stirs anything in me.

As I feel panic begin to seize me, my throat constricting and my hands going numb, a thought occurs to me and I go into the bathroom. I stand in the darkness for a moment, gathering myself, before flicking on the light. At the sight of those blinking eyes, that open mouth, those lips and that hair, I fall to the floor. I am numb everywhere, the blood seeming to leave my body. I clench my arms around my chest and shiver.

There is a voice repeating something over and over. At first it startles me, and I wonder if someone has followed me, or if I turned on the television somehow, but then I realize it is my voice, that my mouth is moving, my tongue and lips forming these words. It does not seem possible. None of this is possible. I know nothing of myself, not my name, who I was, or what I am doing here, but I know, with a certainty so absolute it terrifies me, that the person returning my gaze in the mirror is not me.

2

I crawl from the bathroom, choking back sobs, my whole body shaking with fear and revulsion. I want to peel off this skin, cut off my nose and lips, all of my face. Perhaps beneath it all is the person I am, not this simulacrum. But who is that exactly? I have no sense, no idea of where to even begin. My mind is blank, my thoughts as unfamiliar as the face that stares back at me, though they tantalize at moments, almost seeming to be my own. My instincts have returned me to this place, it is all here somewhere within me. But for now I remain a foreign country to myself.

When I have recovered from my shock enough to get to my feet, I go to the kitchen to see if there is anything to drink. I fumble through the cupboards haphazardly, my search of the apartment only moments before already forgotten, and come across a bottle of rye and some packets of chai tea. I opt for the tea, not trusting my stomach with the alcohol, though the thought of oblivion is tempting. I find the kettle and fill it with water and plug it in, spending a few anxious moments waiting for it to come to a boil.

A phone begins to ring as I wait for the tea to finish

steeping. I locate it in the bedroom atop a dresser amidst a scattering of detritus: loose change, receipts, and sunglasses, all stray pieces of a lost life. Looking at the display I see a name and a number and, while I try to call forth from my memory any details about the Meredith whose name appears there, the call goes to voicemail. The name does not seem familiar to me, but the number is a local one. How I know that I cannot say, but a quick search of the cell for its number shows the same area code. It seems likely that my instincts are correct again.

I nod to myself and go to have my tea, taking the phone with me. Opening up the missed call on the display, I find Meredith's contact and see that the only information I have on her is this phone number. Flipping through the log it appears that she called quite often, every two or three days in most cases. Strangely, or so I think, there are no outgoing calls from this phone to her and no texts in either direction. She is always calling here and the conversations were short, no more than ten minutes. Unusual for a friendship, so an acquaintance, then. But what sort?

Do I dare phone her back in my current state? I need answers, but it is impossible to say whether or not she has any, or whether I can trust her. The fact that there are no outgoing calls or texts to her number seems significant to me. As I mull these questions the phone starts to ring, vibrating insistently on the table. Meredith again. I stare at the display, a hundred competing thoughts racing through my mind, all ending with the face that stared back at me in the mirror and the depthless black that followed.

"Hello," I say, my hands shaking as I hold the phone to my ear.

"Where the hell have you been, David?" says the voice on the other end, without preamble.

"I was out for a walk," I say, after I have recovered from my surprise. My voice, strained and high, filled with tension and adrenaline, sounds more alien than ever to my ears. No more than the name she has just uttered, though, which I immediately feel cannot be mine.

"What a load of..." Her voice trails off in disgust. "Whatever. Look, we need to meet now, as soon as you can."

I hesitate, unsure what to make of her request. Whether due to her manner, or the clear anxiety that underlay it, I do not trust her. But her familiarity, her presumption to ask for a rendezvous, suggests we have done so before. Will refusing strike her as out of character? Will she insist on meeting, or worse, come over to the apartment? I do not want to face her now, not when I am still out of sorts, without any bearings. If I can delay her somehow...She does not give me the chance.

"I don't care if you don't want to," she says, cutting into my silence and reading my thoughts. "We have to meet and we can't afford to wait. They're coming for us. Do you understand? They've found us and they're here."

"Who?" I says, the question sounding stupid, even to my ears.

"What is the matter with you? I'm not talking about this over the phone, for God's sake."

"Sorry, Meredith. You just caught me at a bad time. I'm a little distracted is all."

There is a pause and I can hear her swear under her breath. "Forget about her. We've got bigger problems now. Do you know the Beano?"

"Sure," I say without hesitation, and am startled to realize that I do know exactly the place she is referring to.

"Good. I can be there in ten minutes. You better be there too."

She hangs up before I can say anything further. I hold the phone at my ear, listening to the vacuum on the other end, in a complete daze. At last I set it down and with an unsteady hand take a sip of my now lukewarm tea. *David.* It just doesn't sound right. Nothing felt right about me; it is like an itch I cannot scratch.

There is something not right about Meredith too, I can feel it through the phone. I don't trust her. The threat she mentioned, is that real? It's impossible for me to judge. What seems certain is that she knew plenty about me—the woman she mentioned, for one—and she might very well be able to help with all the questions I have. But do I want to hear the answers?

3

The Cafe Beano is a coffee shop on the corner of a busy avenue not far from the apartment building, a place I am convinced I have been before, though no memory comes to me. Yet I know where it is and can picture its cluttered interior, with tables and chairs strewn about seemingly at random, can smell the bitter coffee and hear the chatter of the menagerie of people gathered within its walls.

It is the specificity of these memories that seems the strangest of all to me. Why can I recall with exacting detail everything about the Beano, but not remember having been there or anywhere else in this city, wherever it is? It's as if someone planted the memory whole within me, but left aside all the context, all the things that make a memory personal. This recollection could be anyone's, just as I could be anyone, and that is what bothers me most of all.

Meredith might be able to help there, I reason, as I walk back through the park to the coffee shop. All those things that seemed so significant earlier—the couple talking, the movement of the light through the tree branches, the damp smell of the earth—I note now in a glancing way, giving them no real thought, my mind on how to proceed with Meredith. Did I reveal to her that I have no memory of who I am? Can I trust her with this information? Best to wait until I better understand what she wants and go from there, I decide.

I have a sudden moment of panic as I step into the Cafe Beano, glancing about at the faces of those sitting at the tables or standing in line for coffee, and realize I have no idea what Meredith looks like. If she is already here I have no way of finding her—how did this not occur to me before, I wonder, feeling my face go red—and there will be no hiding my memory loss from her. Realizing there is nothing else for it now that I am here, I go and stand in line, fidgeting and glancing about to see if anyone in the place is trying to meet my eyes.

As I wait, a slim woman, with hair that wavered between blond and brown, depending on the light, pulled tight into a dancer's bun that peaked atop her head, comes alongside me and says in a quiet voice, so unlike the one she used on the phone, "I'll get a table at the back. Get me a latte."

I nod, our eyes meeting and lingering, before she slips by, disappearing behind me. That brief moment of contact, electric with unspoken thoughts and emotions I cannot even begin to parse, unsettles me deeply. The low level of anxiety I have felt from the moment I stepped into the cafe, overfull with people, talk, and heat, blossoms within me now that this confrontation is at hand.

It is all too much, too quickly. I still haven't recovered from my first glimpse of myself, still do not feel comfortable, even to stand in line, my body, too large or small or just wrong. And now I am out under the unforgiving gaze of others, who I imagine can somehow pierce through whatever disguise I have on and see the falseness at my core.

The woman behind the counter smiles at me as my turn comes to order. "Back already," she says and, when I look at her blankly, adds, "You were just here this morning."

"Right," I say, nodding, not saying anything else and looking away.

The next thing I know I am walking away, coffee in hand. I do not remember ordering or paying, though I must have. My breathing is unsteady and sounds loud in my ears and my hands are numb, so that with each step I worry I will drop the cups. Stopping to gather myself, I see Meredith watching me from a table by the window at the back of the cafe, her face unreadable. The table is near a door leading out to a patio where a few smokers linger, and I note that she will have a clear view of both entrances, as well as the whole of the place. That is not an accident, I think, as I start toward her.

"What is the matter with you?" she says as I sit down. "I thought you were going to faint right there."

I shrug, passing her the latte, and took the lid off mine to blow on it. "Just had a moment."

"What does that mean?" she says, and then waves a hand in exasperation. "Never mind. We've got more important things to talk about."

"You said they were here looking for us?"

Meredith leans forward, her eyes darting around, pitching her voice low. "You remember what I told you about them?"

"Who?" I say automatically, forgetting myself. I flush red, almost wincing as Meredith's steady eyes try to read mine.

"I'm not going to say their name," she says, as though I could not be a greater fool. "You know who. They've brought a Seeker over here."

"Over here?" I say. Something about the way she emphasizes those words draws my attention.

"Here," she says. "If they have a Seeker they will find us. It's a matter of time."

I nod as though I understand. Meredith looks doubtful and she seems about to say something else when her gaze is drawn to the cafe's main entrance. Seeing her eyes transfixed, horror and fear growing in them, I turn to look and see two men standing in the doorway casting their hard eyes around the room as if they are looking for someone.

They are massive in size, tall and broad-shouldered, their muscle evident even beneath the long jackets they wear. Except they are not jackets I notice, as I look closer, more like robes, black in color, except for the red symbol upon the shoulder. Something tugs at my mind as I stare at them, trying to remember where I have seen the figure before, a thought almost taking shape.

It does not come, for the two men step aside and a third comes into view. He is much shorter than they, with a slight build, wearing a similar cut robe, though his is dark grey. His head is almost entirely covered by a grey scarf, the wrapping not unlike that for a turban, leaving only his eyes visible, and those only after a fashion, for he is wearing what appears to be a mutant pair of aviator goggles. The lenses are a deep violet the light reflects strangely off of. It seems impossible that their wearer could see anything out of them. There are no straps extending from the goggles and, as I look closer to determine how they are kept in place, I realize they are fused to his skin in some manner.

As I am wondering how that can be possible, Meredith is standing and taking me by the arm.

"Don't look at them," she whispers, as she pulls me from my chair toward the door. "We have to go."

Dumbfounded by everything that is happening, I let her lead me out the door, though my body feels limp and it is a struggle to move.

"Quickly," Meredith says, her hand pressing hard on my arm as she leads me down the street. "Don't look back."

I am unable to stop myself, though; I have to see the man with the impossible eyes and the robes with the rune I can almost recall having seen before. As I turn to get my last glimpse, Meredith jerking my shoulder hard and swearing at me under her breath, I can just see three of them. They have moved to the center of the cafe, their presence drawing curious stares from those sitting nearby. The man with the grotesque eyes is staring out the window in our direction. I feel a chill run up my spine as I can feel his alien gaze fall upon me.

"They see us," I say to Meredith.

"We'll have to run."

4

Meredith drags me along as she runs, pulling my arm so violently I fear my shoulder might fly from its socket. Behind us I hear a cry in a strange accent, a word I think I know, though I cannot place it. I whisper it to myself as I try to keep up to Meredith and she glares at me furiously, yanking even harder on my arm. The sounds of pursuit grow nearer as we duck around a corner and into a broad alley, weaving around trash dumpsters. One of the pursuers—the man with the goggles, I am certain—utters a command that I cannot make out, and somehow I know they are splitting up to cut off our avenues of escape.

I begin to say something, but Meredith silences me with a glance. Directly in our path are two cooks in stained white jackets outside taking a smoke break, and Meredith heads for them with me in tow. They glance up in surprise at our rapid approach, their astonishment soon replaced by fear as they see the man behind us in pursuit. Their conversation silenced, they watch us, open-mouthed and frozen in place, as Meredith blows past them, carrying me with her. She throws open the door leading into the kitchen, with such violence it almost rebounds off the wall to hit us, and we plunge within before either cook has time to recover and do anything.

Inside we are met by a shout of anger from another cook and a stunned shriek from the waitress we bowl over as we dodge through the galleys. By the time I notice the scalding heat from the ovens hitting my face, we are already out of kitchen, emerging to find ourselves near a bar. A couple, with their arms slung over each other as they lean against the counter, glances up at our sudden entrance. Again I note the long delay before the surprise registers on their faces. Is time moving slower for me, each instant fuller than the last?

I have no time to think about that, for Meredith doesn't pause, flying around the bar, shoving aside anyone who comes near our path, and it is all I can do to keep up with her. The staff is slow to react as well, only moving in our direction when we reach the entrance to the place. By then shouts and cries have begun to arise again from the kitchen and a low murmur of consternation erupts, cut silent by the door swinging shut behind me as we return to the street.

Here Meredith pauses for a second to get her bearings, glancing left and right. My face feels hot and my pulse echoes loudly in my temple. I cannot seem to get enough air into my lungs.

We both see him at the same moment, the dark robe and the flash of scarlet at the shoulder, coming toward us from down the street. Meredith doesn't hesitate, grabbing me by the arm again and leaping into the midst of the traffic passing by in front of us. Instinctively I resist, but she proves surprisingly strong for someone so slight, and easily overpowers me. Once we were in the middle of the street I surrender to her will, trusting she knows what she is doing.

We dart across the rest of the lanes of traffic, the whoosh of air from a passing bus the only blow either of us sustain, and head through the first door we find. The place is a magazine shop, called News of the Day, and we sprint down the narrow aisles teeming with glossy covers. The proprietor does not even look up from where he sits behind the register, his focus entirely on the book he is reading. When we reach the back of the store, near the pornography section, Meredith shoves open the door leading into the back and the man finally realizes something is amiss. He stands up, calling after us as we go, "Excuse me."

Meredith ignores him, slamming the door shut and, after noticing the deadbolt, locking it behind us. She leads me through the dingy back of the store, out into another alley that strangely backs onto another street. There are no storefronts on this avenue, only some parking spaces and, on the far side, an apartment building on one corner, with the rest of the block filled by a park and a lawn bowling club. She heads for the apartment building, angling across the empty street as she goes, moving with ease even as I begin to labor, my lungs burning and sweat streaking my face.

At the door to the apartment building she produces what looks like an uncut key, flat and rectangular, with no grooves carved into it. In spite of its unfinished look it slides easily into the lock, opening the door. Before we enter the building we both, by instinct, look behind to see if anyone is behind us. The street is empty, except for a lone car that passes slowly by, heading in the direction opposite ours. Meredith does not give it more than a glance, before pulling me inside and starting toward the stairs.

"I think we lost them," I venture tentatively.

"No," is her blunt reply, not even bothering to turn to look at me, or slowing her pace whatsoever. I follow behind, my every breath now sounding like a smoker's dying gasp.

At the door to the third floor Meredith stops and turns to me, holding a finger to her lips. While I try valiantly to quiet my breathing, she leads the way forward, going from door to door, holding her head against each one to listen for a moment before moving on. Five apartments in, she finds one to her liking and, slipping the flat key from her pocket, unlocks the door, leading me within. Inside is a spacious apartment, made less so by the two leather couches and a massive flat-screen television in the main room awkwardly filling the space.

"What are we doing here?" I say, as I watch her go from room to room, confirming the apartment is empty.

"Quiet," Meredith says when she is finished her search. "We don't have much time. Take this."

She hands me what I initially think is an overlarge square button. It is cold to the touch and has a weight out of proportion to its size. It is dark and violet, and like the man's goggles, seems to repel light. There are no markings on it, no sign of what purpose it might have. Seeing the perplexed look on my face, Meredith sighs in exasperation and takes the button from me and presses it to the hollow of my neck. To my surprise it sticks to my skin, the cold from it spreading across my throat.

"Not a word," Meredith says, pointing at me. "Not a damn word. Don't move. Don't even breathe."

I do as she says, though I cannot begin to understand why. A few minutes later it becomes all too clear. Down the hall come the voices, those foreign, yet familiar, accents, moving nearer. Soon I can hear their heavy footsteps on the hallway carpet, coming to a halt right before the door to the apartment we have taken refuge in. I take a step back, away from the door and them, not even realizing I have done so. Meredith, her expression colored with fury, clamps her hands on my shoulders and holds me still.

I can almost sense the men pausing on the other side of the door, the moment stretching on and seeming to slow until time went absolutely still. No one seems to breathe as we all wait for something to break the impasse. One of the pursuers whispers something and I feel

Meredith slump a bit in defeat, the air going from her chest in a sigh. The doorknob jiggles and someone fumbles with the lock, while Meredith presses her fingers even more insistently into my arms. The air burns in my lungs and I am afraid to even blink.

A small grunt of triumph is followed by the door swinging open, and the man with the goggles steps into the apartment. He barely glances at the kitchen, moving immediately to the living room where Meredith and I stand. One of the Black Robes follows him partway down the hall, the other staying to keep watch on the corridor. The Seeker, for there seems no doubt who this is, studies the room with a careful disdain. My every instinct cries out for me to find somewhere to hide, but Meredith holds me even tighter, while remaining absolutely still herself.

Though it is impossible, my mind cannot even begin to comprehend it, neither the Seeker nor the Black Robe see us as we stand before them in plain sight. It looks to me as though both of them are staring right at us, yet they notice nothing. How is such a feat achieved? It is the button, I know, but how it can render us invisible I cannot imagine. All I know for certain is that the cold from its heavy substance is spreading from my throat up my cheeks and down to my chest, becoming more painful by the moment.

The Seeker appears to be as confused as I am. He mutters something to himself as he glances around, looking for all the world like someone who has misplaced his keys. Though I do not catch what he says I am certain he is speaking English, which surprises me for some reason. It does not seem possible that someone so strange and alien looking would have English as his native tongue. But there is much about the world that does not seem possible at this very moment.

Each time he casts his gaze about the room he returns to stare directly at me, as though he somehow knows that we are there in spite of what his eyes tell him. As I watch him I realize that he is not staring at the two of us, but at the place I was standing before my inadvertent step. He studies that space for what seems minutes, not moving at all.

The spreading cold from the button makes me want to shiver, and it soon becomes an irresistible sensation that takes all my will not to give in to. I take half-breaths through my nose, terrified that even that slight stirring of the air will attract the Seeker's attention. His eyes are even more fearsome to look at up close, for they are not quite like the aviator goggles I have in my head, but more like an insect's eyes viewed up close with a thousand tiny hexagons linking together to form those opaque and impenetrable circles. From a distance they looked constructed, a clumsy addition made to human flesh, but now I am certain they are organic, and a part of him, cell placed upon cell forming this monstrous whole.

The Black Robe in the hallway shifts his weight and the Seeker glances toward him and nods, as though acknowledging the search has come to an end. He turns back to where Meredith I stand and whispers something, his voice pitched so that only someone very near him, as we were, can hear it. The hairs stand on the back of my neck at the phrase, whether from the tone of his voice or some innate understanding of what the words mean. But, try as I might, I cannot recall the words. Meredith, I notice with some curiosity, stiffens at them, as though fighting the urge to reply in kind.

The Seeker's words seem to hang in the air like a threat, until he shakes his head and turns away from where we stand, heading out of the apartment. The Black Robes follow behind, one of them shutting the door. As the sound of their footsteps down the hall disappears, both of us exhale at the same moment, Meredith's breath warm on my ear. I can feel her hands trembling on my arms and neither of us dares to move for a long while.

5

Meredith is the first to move, releasing her grip on my arms and plucking the button from my neck. She returns it and the one she wore to her jacket pocket while I rub my throat, the cold gradually receding from my skin. I am giddy with relief at our apparent escape and have a thousand questions, but Meredith's face is marked by a coiled sort of anger that warns me from asking any of them just now.

By the time we leave the apartment, nightfall approaches, the sun low in the sky and the shadows long. We slip out the back into a taxi Meredith has called. She sends the driver on a circuitous route, watching out the back window for the entire trip, with the same grim expression on her face. When she is satisfied we have not been followed, she directs him to an apartment building called the Ivanhoe, an older brick building in a neighborhood I think is near to my own. Each floor, I note as we ascend up the stairs to the fifth, has a slightly unpleasant odor in its hallway, all of them distinct from the others somehow.

The apartment that Meredith brings me to is cramped and narrow, filled with ornate antique furniture too large for its rooms, forcing us to navigate with care in order to move about the place. There are shelves heavy with books, some of them very old, and the air is dense with the smell of them. Everything here seems to run counter to the person I met this afternoon; it has none of Meredith's care or precision.

Seeing the look on my face, Meredith says, "It's a friend's. Someone they couldn't possibly know, so it should take them awhile to find us again."

"How long?"

"We can spend the night."

What happens after that, she leaves unsaid. She tells me to sit and make myself comfortable while she gets us something to eat, which I try to do, though I am seized by a restlessness that will not quiet. All the tension and fear of the day, which at times seemed remote, even when the Seeker was staring directly at me and our discovery seemed imminent, collapses upon me now the danger is past. As smells of the meal Meredith is preparing waft over to me, I try to steady myself by staring out the window to watch the sun descending, bathing the city's downtown in fiery purples and reds.

A sense of hopelessness seizes me, the little that I know, and the vast ocean of all I do not, utterly overwhelming me. The wrongness of myself, of this body, resurfaces now that I am left alone with my thoughts, and I want nothing more than to lie on the couch and sob. I know I cannot, though, not while Meredith is here. Until I have a better sense of what is happening and of who I am, I cannot trust her or anyone. There are too many mysteries and, to this point, no answers, beyond the fact that my life is in danger.

Though I can still remember nothing of my past, the world seems to me no longer the one I had known. Men with insect eyes who can find me seemingly at will. Buttons that hide people in plain sight. Languages and symbols unlike anything I have seen or heard. It is all too much to process, on top of everything else I am dealing with. And yet from moment to moment I have the sense that it is all there, all the understanding and knowledge I need is somewhere in my mind, always slipping just beyond my grasp.

Meredith brings me our supper—mushroom soup and toast—and we eat in silence, both of us uneasy in the other's presence. I cannot even begin to think of what I might say, where to begin with all that has occurred. The food pushes aside all such worries, for I am ravenous beyond belief, unsurprising given that I have no idea when I have last eaten. When we are both done I do the dishes, enjoying the simplicity of the task and the distraction it provides.

I return to the living room when I am done, where Meredith sits on the couch, her legs curled up underneath her, a book on her lap. "It's about religion," she says, noticing my interest, "My friend studies it."

"All religion. Or a religion?"

"Well, he's interested in the philosophy, I guess, and the history of them."

"Trying to find the right one," I say, trying and failing to sound lighthearted.

Meredith shrugs. "Aren't we all." She sets the book aside and motions for me to sit down. "How are you feeling? I know it was probably not the day you were expecting."

"No," I say, "I guess not."

She looks away from me, hesitating again, staring at the darkness beyond the window. "How much do you remember?"

"What do you mean?" I say, smiling, even as my heart begins to race and sweat gathers on my palms. What can I tell her that might make any sense?

"No," she says. "I need to know for sure. The Seeker will not stop, he will find us, and we'll need to be prepared. Do you remember anything at all?"

She looks at me, concern etched upon her face, yet all I can think is that she knows what the Seeker whispered in the apartment. She has the buttons. None of the day's events prove that she is any more trustworthy than the Seeker and his minions. There is something about her that makes me question her motives. The concern on her face, the emotion in her eyes, it all feels false somehow. But I have no other choice.

"No," I say, "I don't remember anything before this afternoon."

6

My words hang in the air, the silence growing uncomfortable as we both avoid each other's gaze, unsure of how to proceed. After the momentary relief of my confession, the need to carry on with the poor charade I attempted now obviated, my unease returns in full force. My future is now tied to Meredith, and a precarious future it is with the specter of the Seeker looming on every horizon. I have no way to tell whether the trust I have given her was earned.

"I'm going to make some tea," she says. "Would you like some? This could take awhile."

"Sure," I say, glad for the distraction. It is good to have something in my hands, something to do, otherwise I keep twitching my fingers, touching them together in weird patterns to get the feel and sense of them. Nothing about them feels like my own. While Meredith is making the tea I wander about the apartment, picking up books off the shelves and glancing at them. All of them are about various religions, origins and histories, anthropologies and comparative studies. The words become a blur after a time.

When the tea is ready we sit beside each other on the

couch again, Meredith curling her legs underneath her and wrapping both hands around the steaming cup. We are near enough to touch one another and her closeness feels deliberate, an attempt to establish a rapport with me. I tell myself I am being unfair, that it is just my own discomfort, the totality of my confusion, which makes me suspect her of manipulating me.

"This isn't the first time this has happened," Meredith says, blowing on her tea. I feel my hands tremble at her words, my whole body seeming to go cold.

"When was the first time?"

Meredith thought a moment. "Around eight months ago. And a year before that, right when you met Laila."

The name felt familiar in a way Meredith's never had. "Laila," I say, savoring the sound of the name.

"Yes," Meredith says darkly, watching my reaction. "She was trouble."

I look at her, a question in my eyes, and she waves her hand. "It's not my place. I shouldn't have said anything."

"Okay," I say, my voice sounding higher than I would like. "So if this has happened before, I should get my memory back."

"Yes," Meredith says, though she doesn't sound convinced. "You did before," she adds when she sees my face fall. "But it wasn't a simple thing and it didn't all come back. Less each time, actually."

"What did I do to get it back?" I say, trying not to let my desperation show.

"We tried a lot of things. I'm not sure any of them worked. Time, I think, is the only thing, and we don't have any right now."

"Because of the Seeker?"

"Yes," Meredith says. She seems to go very still at the word, watching me carefully to gauge my reactions.

"Do we know what caused it?" I say.

"We were never sure what the cause was," she says, hesitating for a moment before continuing, "Look, you should know that you and I were never close. We were not friends here. We were colleagues. So you may have known better than I do what caused it and how to fix it. But you didn't tell me."

"Colleagues?"

"In a manner of speaking. Friends of convenience. Is that better? I don't know," Meredith says. I shrug and Meredith gets up and begins to pace a cramped path through the living room. I watch her, unsure what to say or do. She stops, as if realizing what she is doing, and forces herself to sit down.

"I'm sorry, I can't deal with this right now," she says, waving her hands in my direction. "If we had more time…But we need to figure out what we're doing.

"I don't know how to explain it," she says, anticipating my questions. "The world is not as it seems."

"Evidently," I say, wondering why she is so nervous now, after all that has happened. "Why don't we start with the men who found us. How did they and why were they looking in the first place?"

"Right. Okay." She takes a deep breath. "The Seeker found us. Some call them Finders. They have a Society, like a guild, you know. People hire them when they want someone found."

Doubt fills my thoughts and, I'm sure, is evident on my face. What knowledge I have of the world in my current state does not include men like the Seeker or artifacts like the button. It is a world of certain laws, and though I have witnessed these things in action, my mind still rebels against their very existence.

"Look," Meredith says, reaching out to put a hand on my knee. "I know this sounds incredible. There's no way I can prove anything to you, you'll just have to trust me. You have to trust someone, and I did save us from the Seeker."

"Then try to explain it to me. Those people, whoever they are, where did they come from?"

"Like I said, the world is not what it seems. There's more than one actually. And the Seeker and the people who hired them came from one of the other ones."

"And we come from that world too," I say. The button she used, as well as the fact that on some level I knew the words the Speaker whispered tells me as much.

"It's more complicated than that," Meredith says, "but yes, we do. Like I said, there are many worlds—universes—and we've ended up in this one. And now someone is looking for us."

"Do you know who?"

"I can guess. We're not here by choice, you and I. We're living in exile, I guess you could say. You see, all the worlds, the universes, are the same, but different, and there are an infinite number."

"Parallel universes," I say to her, the words materializing from somewhere.

"Yes. Exactly. There are versions of you and I in each of them, with different lives, different histories. The worlds in them are different as well. In some, life isn't even possible and we never existed. Some are more or less the same as this, where people aren't even aware of the other worlds. Some have advanced tech, like the Seekers, and have figured out how to travel between the universes. There was a battle over that, over who should be able to travel between. Our side lost and we were trapped here."

I nod as though I understand, but I just feel dizzy. It all feels so unbelievable and the way Meredith tells it, so hesitant, choosing her words with such care, makes me think that whatever truth might be there is only a part of the whole, the rest still to be revealed. One part does ring true, though, that I am not of this place. Maybe that accounts for my sense of dislocation, the itch that works at my being, the wound that is my flesh. Meredith, I see, is watching me, a guarded expression on her face, waiting to see if I will accept all that she has told me.

"Why are these people after us now?"

Something like a sigh of relief escapes her lips. "I don't know. They call themselves the Society of Travelers. They were a guild, like the Seekers, but now they are much more powerful. They essentially rule the world we come from."

"Because they control the gateways between the universes?"

"Yes," Meredith says. "None but them shall pass. The penalty is death for people, like us, who've gone through without their authority. What I don't understand is how they could know we're here now. It makes no sense. Something must have happened, but I can't imagine what."

"So they'll kill us once they find us." The words, the thought itself, should invoke terror in me, but I feel nothing.

"Eventually. They'll want to find out why we're here and what we know first."

"And what do we know?"

Meredith shrugs. "Nothing that would be of interest to them." Something about the way she says that gives me pause, and for some reason I recall the Seeker's whispered threat.

"But there must be something we know, something about us that makes us a threat. They can't just kill us for no reason."

This sparks something within her and she responds vehemently. "No, you don't know them. They don't need a reason. They will hunt us down until none of us is left. And there's nothing you or I can do. They won't stop, and we can't expect any help. We've been forgotten by the people who sent us here."

I am taken aback by the bitterness in her voice and left unsure as to how to respond. Meredith does not give me a chance to, standing up and saying, "I'm sorry. I shouldn't be putting my burdens on you. Not when you're in this state. We should go to bed. We can talk more in the morning and figure out what we're going to do."

I nod my agreement and offer to sleep on the couch, but she points to the bedroom. "No, you've been through more than me today. Besides, this is more my size anyway."

I do not offer any more protest, for as soon as she mentioned sleep, the exhaustion I have been struggling to hold at bay overwhelms me. I throw myself upon the bed, not even bothering to take off my clothes or crawl beneath the covers. In spite of how tired I am, my thoughts won't allow me to sleep, my mind continuing to reflect upon all that Meredith said. Every expression, every pause she took, seems a portent of some deeper truth that, as yet, eludes me.

The thought that keeps returning is about our having been forgotten by those who sent us here. Something about that doesn't ring true. How did she know the Seeker had arrived without someone sending her a message? There are explanations she could offer, no doubt, but I suspect I would find them no more convincing than anything else she said. I am the only forgotten one here, cast adrift from my person, without any bearings, and nothing to hold on to in a world that is growing more turbulent by the moment.

7

It feels like hours before I fall asleep. Outside the room I can hear Meredith pacing about the apartment and, though I do not hear her voice, I am certain she is speaking with someone. Why I should feel this way I cannot say, but it is of a piece with the rest of the inexplicable day. Multiple universes. Seekers. Hidden Societies and secret wars. I have no idea who I am, what city, or indeed what world, I am in, and each of Meredith's revelations offers no solid ground on which I can stand.

The crux of the matter, it seems to me, lies in Meredith's identity and her relationship with me. *Friends of convenience*, she said. *Acquaintances*. What do these things mean and why do I continually feel she is lying to me? All that she told me to this point fits the facts as best I understand them, though that understanding is deeply influenced by Meredith herself, and she saved me from the Seeker. I am under no illusions as to his intent, or his otherworldly nature, after our encounter this afternoon. Still, I can't bring myself to trust her. Who is she and why is she involved in my life?

If I can only remember something of myself. It is strange to me that I know the fundamental laws of this world and have an understanding of how things should be here, yet I know nothing of these other universes. Meredith told me I come from another universe—should I not possess the same basic understanding of it, of all of this? Nothing makes sense, nothing seems right, and I have no idea what to believe.

Sleep comes eventually, but my confused state remains, pursuing me into my dreams. In them I am being hunted by hundreds of insect-eyed men. They are everywhere I turn, and no matter where I try to hide myself they can see me. One moment I am in a forest of dandelion-like flowers, their heads white with long, spindly seeds that rattle in the wind. The next I am deep underground, in a vast, empty complex, my footsteps echoing down the metallic corridors. As I scurry through these strange places, twisting and turning, doubling back on my path, the army of Seekers always discovering me regardless, I find myself wondering if these places are real. Are they a part of another universe that I have been to before?

My endless flight comes to an end at my apartment. I go from room to room, rifling through drawers and lifting up furniture, knocking on the walls to see if there are false panels. Soon I am in a frenzy, tearing apart my bed and the cushions on the couch. Nothing is revealed, nor do I have any sense of what it is I am looking for, only that it is somewhere in the apartment. At last, exhausted by my efforts, I collapse to the floor and begin to sob. I have to remember, my very life is at stake, but I cannot. What has happened to me?

When I have cried until my eyes ache and my throat is raw, I gather myself and go to the bathroom. The face, puffy and red from crying, that looks back at me is not the one I saw this morning. I stare at it, trying to memorize every contour, but the visage dissolves as soon as it takes form in my thoughts. Growing frustrated by my inability to remember, I look down at the sink, trying to steady myself, and when I look up again my true face is gone and the face staring back at me is the false one.

I react to this with fury, slamming my fist into the mirror until it cracks, rendering my countenance into ghoulish carnival forms. A trail of blood flowing into the sink alerts me to the cuts on my hand. When I hold it to my eyes I can see the white of bone and nearly faint. I reach out to steady myself on the sink counter, the pain from my hand bludgeoning me, sending the room spinning. I lose all equilibrium and fall to the floor and into darkness.

A hand, gentle on my shoulder, stirs me awake. For a moment I do not remember where I am, but, as I blink my eyes open, I recognize, in the dim light of the dawn coming through the shades, the bedroom of Meredith's friend. I roll over, expecting to see Meredith, only to be brought face to face with the Seeker, his strange eyes two pits of blackness in the shadows.

I try to scream but no sound comes from my throat. The Seeker makes no move to seize me, merely considering me, his head cocked to the side. His manner, like a scientist viewing a specimen, leaves me unable to react as I await the scalpel's edge. When at last he stirs, it is to gesture toward the door for me to go. I do not move, still paralyzed by his sudden appearance, and he gestures again, uttering the same phrase he earlier whispered to the air, while we remained hidden from his sight.

I recognize the words, yet their meaning escapes my conscious thought, dissolving as my true face dissolved before the form grew solid. They seem to break the spell I am under, though, and I climb from the bed and go out into the main room, only to find I have somehow returned to my own apartment. I feel lost and thick-headed. The Seeker prods me into the living room, not giving me time to sort through my confusion. There he gestures for me to sit in a chair facing out to the balcony, while he sits on the couch alongside.

"It is good to see you again." The voice comes from behind me. It is a calm, unemotional voice. A man's. I try to turn around, but am unable to. The chair has seized me, holding my neck and arms in a vise, though no bonds are visible to my eyes.

"Still looking, I see," the voice says, with a hint of amusement, and I follow his unseen gesture and see my apartment in ruins from my earlier futile excavations. Where have I heard him before? Try as I might, I cannot picture his face.

"You should have known, after all we have been through, that you could not defy me," he says, and I imagine him shaking his head, almost in sorrow. "A price must be incurred."

This infuriates me for some reason, and I fight against the invisible bonds in a frenzy. My mouth is open to reply when I awake to find myself in Meredith's friend's bedroom, the sheets tangled about me.

8

I lie still for several moments as I try to judge whether I am still in the midst of a dream or truly awake. My utter exhaustion, and the sense that I have not slept at all, decides it for me. It is impossible, I think, to be this tired in a dream. The smell of instant oatmeal and coffee reaches my nostrils, stirring my stomach and driving me from bed. I find Meredith in the kitchen, sitting at the small table eating the oatmeal she has prepared.

"Coffee's on and there's more porridge. Might be cereal too, if that's more your thing. Eat quick, we don't have much time."

I nod, not bothering to reply, my mind still mired in a fog. After I have finished with my breakfast, she hands me a toothbrush and toothpaste, still in their packaging. I stare, wondering how she could have known to bring it with her yesterday.

"I picked it up first thing this morning," she says. "If you want a shower, be quick. I want to be out of here in the next half-hour."

We are out the door before eight, Meredith alert and watchful as we go down the stairs, while I still feel groggy and unable to fully awaken. We arrive at the Ivanhoe's entrance just as a vehicle pulls to a stop in the loading zone out front. Even in the dim morning light, clouds heavy with rain obscuring the sky above, I can see the stern-faced Black Robes. I gasp aloud, the fog in my mind lifting in an instant, though it is replaced by a terrified paralysis that leaves me standing exposed in the foyer.

The arrival of our hunters has not escaped Meredith's notice; she shoves me against the wall as she digs into her jacket, pulling out the two buttons we used yesterday. I reach out to take one from her, but she brushes my hand away and sets them on the floor by our feet. We stand by them for several agonizing seconds as I watch the Black Robes get out of their silver car, before fleeing back down the hallway to the building's rear entrance and into the alley. With Meredith in the lead, we run to the narrow lane that cuts between the buildings opposite the Ivanhoe, cross the street, and go between two more apartment complexes.

The ground slopes sharply, and I nearly tumble headlong into Meredith, catching myself just in time. There is a wooden slat fence behind the apartments, running alongside the alley atop a retaining wall, leaving a steep drop to a pathway below. Meredith does not break from her loping pace as she comes to the fence, pulling herself up and over in one smooth motion. She drops down to the pathway below, disappearing from my sight. I stop as I come to the fence, which rises up well above my head, unsure of how to get myself over it in this body that feels so unfamiliar.

"Come on," Meredith hisses to me from where she crouches, the urgency in her voice doing nothing to alleviate my anxiety.

I glance over my shoulder to assure myself that no pursuit has arrived and see only a woman, in a faded pare of pajamas, watching me with some curiosity from her balcony. That spurs me to action. I clamber up the side of the fence, awkwardly swinging one leg after the other over, and slide down so only my fingertips are touching its top. At that point I let go, landing heavily on the ground and stumbling backwards, wrenching my ankle in the process. Meredith stares at me, amazed at my clumsiness, and shakes her head before starting down the alley at a trot.

We emerge onto another sleepy street and Meredith slows her pace to a brisk walk, pulling me up alongside her so that we look like a couple out for morning stroll. I feel as though people are watching us from every window and balcony, each parked car filled with Black Robes waiting to signal to the Seeker. I cannot resist looking around to confirm my suspicions.

Meredith squeezes my hand hard, causing me to grimace. "Stop it," she says with a glare. "Just look straight ahead."

I force myself to follow her orders, keeping my head down and my eyes upon the square of concrete just ahead of my feet. We walk to the end of the block and turn the corner onto another innocuous street, this one ending at a large apartment complex that runs for most of the block on the street perpendicular to the one we are on. There are no cars or people about, the only sound reaching my ears the hum of traffic somewhere in the distance. But the calm seems deceptive, a trick of nature designed to ensnare me.

Meredith appears unconcerned and she leads me by the arm down the gravel driveway at the same easy, maddening pace, my whole being crying out that we should be running, though where I can't say.

Sensing my distress, Meredith says, "They don't know what we look like and they didn't get a good look at us yesterday. So just don't draw attention and we'll be fine."

How this can be possible when the Seeker had, as befitted his name, unerringly found us, after we lost the Black Robes in our mad dash yesterday, I cannot say. But I force myself to relax. I have no choice but to trust her for now.

The driveway curves around the building, leading to the

car park at the back. Alongside it is a patch of indifferently cared for grass extending to some overgrown bushes and trees that crowd over a thin path, worn by many feet. It is that path we set upon, turning from the driveway, passing through a natural gateway provided by the shrubbery.

On the other side we find ourselves at a stairway that descends to a busy street below. Two stone Victorian lions look out on the passing cars at the bottom of the staircase, their visages worn away by the passing years. I run my hand along the nearest as we pass by, wondering what magnificent building once sat above, of which no remaining signs can be seen. It feels as though we have passed from one world into another.

At the end of the block there is a bus stop with a large shelter to provide cover from the rain, and it is here that Meredith goes, ducking within and handing me some change, saying, "Make sure you ask for two zones."

I stare at the coins in my hand, dumbfounded. "What are we doing?"

Meredith pulls a cell phone from her jacket, glancing at the display. "We have time."

"How do you know?" I say, nonplussed. "What if the bus is late?"

"It won't matter," she says. "We have time."

Before I can interrogate her further, an elderly woman steps into the shelter, nodding at both of us. Meredith smiles in return and turns her attention to the road, watching for the bus, glancing every now and again down at her phone. I catch a glimpse of the display and see the outlines of what I think is a map, the gridlines of the city apparent. The colors and outlines on it are strange, and it seems as though there is a map imposed on another map, a city upon the city in effect, which I can make no sense of.

The minutes tick by as we wait for the arrival of the bus, traffic ebbing and flowing on the road, a few more people trickling into our shelter. Though Meredith continues to exude calm, it has no effect on me. I keep waiting for the arrival of the Black Robes, for the Seeker to appear behind me as in my dream, and the voice, mocking and precise, to cut into me. None of that occurs. The day remains ordinary and we appear ordinary within it.

When the bus pulls up, lurching to a stop, I feel no relief, my agitation blossoming within me as we start on the next leg of our journey. This is no way to escape a dire threat, it seems to me. Meredith looks unconcerned, staring at the road ahead, the phone returned to her pocket. When I feel as though I can't breath any longer, I turn to her and say, "How are we supposed to get away from these people taking a bus if they can find us wherever we go?"

She considers the question, her eyes darting around to see if anyone is paying attention. "They will find us, but it takes time. Remember, they haven't got a good look at us yet, and they don't know our names, or anything about our lives here. They have to rely on the Seeker, and he is an imprecise tool."

"How do they not know what we look like?"

"They don't. They never do. That is why they have the Seeker."

"But they saw us yesterday," I say, my voice going louder than I intended.

Meredith glares at me. "But how good of a look did they get? We were running, so it was obvious who they should be chasing. But could they pick us out of a crowd again if we were acting normally? I don't think so."

"So why did we run yesterday?"

"Because you looked back," Meredith says, standing up to get off the bus. As we disembark, she glances at her phone and a small grimace passes across her face, vanishing by the time we are on the sidewalk. A metro line crosses directly overhead of the bus stop, and Meredith heads for the stairway leading to the station.

"Why not use the buttons again?" I say as we go up the stairs.

Meredith glances at me. "You mean the stealth? They were expecting us to. That's why I left them in the hallway. It should have taken them awhile to figure out that we aren't there."

"But it didn't," I say, my voice catching.

"No," she says, glancing at her phone again as we come up into the station. "They're very close now."

The metro station consists of a long platform, raised above the street, with tracks running on either side. It is filled with morning commuters, bleary-eyed and grim-faced, peering at their phones or staring off at nothing. Nobody gives us so much as a glance as we weave through the crowd, finding some empty space toward the middle of the platform. Meredith pulls out her phone and winces at what she sees.

"Take out your phone," she says under her breath, not even glancing over at me. "Act like you're doing something with it."

I do as she says, scrolling through my text messages, pretending I am looking for something. A name catches my eye as I go. *Laila*. Meredith mentioned her. I open her thread thinking I will read what we texted to each other.

"Now, pay attention," Meredith says, moving behind me and turning so our backs face. "Whatever you do, don't stop looking at your screen. They're going to be here in a second, so if you notice them, don't stare and don't run. Just keep looking at your phone, and when the train comes, get on it."

I nod and then, realizing Meredith can't see me, say, "Okay."

"It's better if we're not together," Meredith continues. "So I'm going to go stand farther down the platform. It will take them longer to find us that way. Don't look for me. Don't worry about me. Just get on the train when it comes."

I let out an unsteady breath as I feel her slip away from behind me, moving down the platform to my left. A train arrives behind me and, by reflex, I glance up as the line and destination are announced. The crowd swirls around me as people get on and off the train. I try not to look at anyone as they brush past, a blur of faces, all without expression. Somehow they all seem sinister for it, malevolent in their ignorance. It is an effort to force myself to breathe.

A low murmur, passing along the platform like a wave approaching the shore, alerts me to the arrival of the Black Robes and the Seeker. I close my eyes and bite my tongue, anything to distract me from the overwhelming urge to turn and see where they are. The screen to my phone has gone dark and I turn it on again, going back to Laila's messages, forcing myself to read them, to think about what they say. It is no use, the words are a blur, and I stop even trying as the murmur grows closer and closer, until it is very near, right around me.

My every instinct is to look up at what I know is there, but I do not, keeping my eyes trained just above the display of my phone, so that I can see to the platform's edge. The Seeker passes in front of me a moment later, drawing stares from many in the crowd. He goes slowly, glancing from face to face, meeting all the stares that he draws. Just as I think he is going to pass by, to keep going down the platform, he stops, lifting his head, as though testing the air for a scent.

Where, I wonder, is the damn train? The Seeker stays where he is, glancing around, his head cocked expectantly. Though I want to look around myself, to see where the Black Robes are, to see where Meredith is, I force myself to stay as I am, utterly still. I do not even look at the Seeker, staring intently at my phone, only his legs visible in my sight line. He takes a step forward and I nearly sag with relief, until he stops again. I think I see him raise his hand, as though to beckon someone to him, but I dare not look up to confirm.

Two trains arrive, almost simultaneously, and the

platform becomes a mass of confusion as the doors open and people pour off and on both lines at once. The train in front of me is full already, and I push my way forward, panicked that I won't be able to make it on. I do not even look to see if the Seeker, the Black Robes, or Meredith join me as I shove my way on, drawing a few looks of ire from my fellow passengers.

When I am safely on, I allow myself a glance out at the platform and see the Seeker in the midst of the crowd looking at the train, at the very car I am in. My heart goes still and I try to will the doors shut and start the train moving. For an agonizing moment our eyes met and linger, the door open and the train still. An announcement breaks the spell, both of us glancing toward the speaker at the sound. The doors hiss and slide close and the train lurches forward, carrying me on and leaving the Seeker behind.

9

The tension does not leave me as the platform disappears from view, replaced by a checkerboard vista of streets filled with houses, stretching on for what seems an endless distance. The people around me on the train seem to press closer and closer, especially after the next stop as more passengers get on. I shudder at their inadvertent touch, wanting to shove back at those whose arms and backs are pressed against mine. *My life is in danger*, I want to cry out. The dull and distant expressions on everyone's faces tell me how that will be received. I will just be another of the train's discomforts that has to be endured.

My phone vibrates in my hand, a text from Meredith: *In the next car. Did you get on all right?*

Yes. But the Seeker saw me, I reply.

Her reply, instantaneous, hints at her anxiety: *Did they get on the train?*

I tell her they did not, my hands shaking as I tap at the phone. My face feels flush and feverish, my forehead damp with sweat. There is a knot in my stomach, clenching and unclenching. I begin to worry that the other passengers are watching me, noticing my distress, and wondering what is wrong with me.

The phone vibrates again. *Good*, Meredith says. *We're riding to the end of the line.* I glance up at the transit map above the door and count the stops left—five, it appears—and try to focus on my breathing. I relax, ignoring everyone around me, being pushed and pulled as though I am adrift at sea, without purpose.

My mind will not stay quiet for long, the lingering glance of the Seeker resurfacing in my thoughts. What was he thinking in that moment? If I were to guess I would say that he is indifferent to my escape. There is patience there, a knowledge of an inevitable conclusion. In due time he will run me to ground. I feel that inevitability as well. Even if we manage to slip this particular chase, we will have to stop at some point and he will find us again, just as he did this morning. There seems no point in running, which makes me wonder why Meredith is. She knows how hopeless our situation was. Unless there is something she is not telling me.

After the second stop, the train drops from its perch above the streets and enters a tunnel. The closing off of the view only serves to deepen my despair, so that by the time the train reaches the end of the line I am prepared to simply wait upon the platform for the Black Robes to come and seize me. Why prolong this misery further? I do not know who I am, cannot begin to understand the situation I find myself in, and I have no hope of escape.

Meredith intuits my desperation when she finds me in the swirling mass of people entering and exiting the train. She grabs me by the arm, pulling me forward. "What's the matter?" she hisses in my ear.

"Why run?" I say to her, paying no attention to where she is leading me. "They're just going to find us again, right?"

"Maybe," she says. "But we can't face them here."

"We can't do anything to stop them, can we?" I say, shrugging off her arm and stopping. "The men with the Seeker are trained, aren't they? They can handle us easily.

The Seeker too."

Meredith turns and looks at me, and for once I see her true face, lined with worry and doubt. "Look," she says, "this is bad. There's no doubt. I don't know if we can survive. Maybe if you had your memory back. Maybe. But we can't do anything here. Our only hope is to keep moving. There's a place. If we can get there, we have a chance."

"What chance is that?"

"I don't know," she says. "But we have to try."

She turns and walks away, heading toward the harbor front, where a small ferry is docked. "Come on," she says, not even bothering to look back to see if I am coming. Her bluff has the desired effect and I set off after her. What else can I do after all, but try and hope that my memory returns to me in time?

The ferry takes us across the bay to the north side of the city. We disembark at a busy pier, filled with restaurants, bars and tourist shops, all housed in a single complex that looks out across the water at downtown. Meredith leads me through the complex, glancing at the various food stands as though she is deciding what she wants to eat. Behind the dockside building is a former warehouse that has been converted into a farmer's market, crammed with produce stands. Even though it is early in the morning, the place is filled with people.

We join the flow of people as they move through the stalls, Meredith seeming to be in no rush, which I find strange given we have only a five- to ten-minute lead on the Seeker, assuming he has taken the next train. She glances at her phone as we go, nodding to herself, and says to me, "There is someone here who can help us. Keep your eyes out for the glassworks. His place is beside it."

I nod, joining her in looking from side to side. We come to end of the warehouse and turn to go down the next aisle. There is a door open to the street and a grey van is parked at an odd angle outside, hazard lights blinking.

Something about is out of place, and I stop for a moment to look at it. A busy cafe occupies the corner of the warehouse and people crowd around, as they wait for their coffee and pastries, or try to decipher the handwritten menu on the chalkboard above the stand.

Just as I start forward, pushing the van from my mind, a large group of people come around the corner, cutting into the flow of traffic and separating me further from Meredith, who has her eyes on her phone. She hasn't noticed that I have stopped, and I am about to call out to her when a hand clenches around my throat and what feels like the barrel of a gun is pressed against my back.

"You're coming with me," a man says.

TWO:

THE CHURCH OF THE REGENTS

10

"Not a word," the man says, his breath moist on my ear, as he guides me through the crowd toward the warehouse door. He removes his hand from my throat, but the gun remains pressed against my back. I crane my head as we go, trying to catch Meredith's eye before I disappear. It has only taken an instant for us to be separated and the man to intercept me, though it feels as though minutes are passing with each breath. I catch sight of Meredith as we come to the door, frantically scanning the crowd trying to find me, and I open my mouth to call out to her.

"Don't even think about it," the man says, grabbing my arm and brutally wrenching it, causing me to gasp in pain.

He shoves me out the door just as I think I see her catching sight of me with my assailant, a look of horror on her face. That is the last I see of her, for as we step outside the back door to the van is thrown open and two others emerge, seizing my arms and dragging me within. The first assailant shuts the door behind them and gets into the front passenger seat just as the van starts to drive away.

The sudden motion of the van sends me tumbling forward onto my stomach, and one of the two kidnappers jumps on top me, pinning me to the floor of the van as the other tightens a plastic zip tie around my wrists. When I am secured to their satisfaction, they sit on either side of me, watching with some amusement as I struggle to turn myself over. I end up with my back against the metal divider that separates us from the front of the van, creating a rear compartment sealed entirely from the outside world. There are no windows and the only illumination is provided by a square bulb at the center of the roof. It is also the only furnishing, the walls and floor bare metal.

The van takes a left and then a hard right and begins to pick up speed, spilling me onto my side in the process. After I have righted myself again, I turn my attention to my captors. One is a woman and the other a man, both blank-faced and nondescript. By the set of their shoulders I guess they are capable of handling themselves in a way I clearly am not. Neither of them so much as glances at me, nor did they say anything to each other.

I try to think of something to say to break the silence, perhaps draw them out and determine who they are. I have to assume they are a new entrant to the field of those interested in my lost self. The look on their faces tells me that conversation would not be advisable, and nothing comes to mind that would lead to any fruitful discussion on the matter of my kidnapping, so I keep my counsel for the moment. The van takes some more turns, but I stop paying attention, having no sense of what direction we are going.

Our journey does not last long, no more than fifteen minutes by my best estimate, each more agonizing than the last. The grim silence and emotionless expressions of my assailants feel more and more ominous as my mind, left to its own devices, begins to imagine the increasingly elaborate torture I am about to be subjected to. The woman, perhaps sensing my growing distress, looks at me from the corner of her eyes and smirks, the mocking grin vanishing when the man sees it and glares at her, both resuming their stony countenances. I have a sudden, desperate urge to urinate, my bladder aching and my legs trembling as I fight to keep control of my body and avoid that final humiliation.

I am so focused on my fear of soiling myself I fail to notice the van has come to a halt, until the woman gets up to the open the door. The man drags me from its confines, not caring when I hit my head on the roof. We are parked in an alley outside a bland suburban office building whose windows are dark. I think about crying out to see if anyone is nearby, but both the man and the woman seize me firmly by the arms and the thought makes me cringe, knowing they will not hesitate to inflict some damage upon me if I make any attempt to call for help. The driver and the man who took me from the market fall in behind, no one speaking as we enter via the loading dock, someone inside buzzing us in.

As with the van, the building's interior is stripped bare; even the doors have been taken from their hinges, leaving only empty rooms and bare walls. There is the odd bit of refuse inexplicably left behind that hints at the former life of the place: a pile of keyboards in a corner here, a cubicle wall in the middle of the floor there, and a box full of pens and staplers thrown at random in another room. These accoutrements of a mundane past only add to my growing sense of horror as we move into the center of the building near the elevators, which stand open-mouthed and leering at our passage.

The wrongness of the place is confirmed as we come to a room that does have a door. It is heavy looking and impenetrable, having clearly been added after the building was gutted, no doubt by its present occupants. A keypad is mounted on the wall beside the door and the woman punches in a code, the buttons producing odd tones. Air hisses out as the door unlocks and slides open and I am dragged within.

The atmosphere in the room is of a hospital, arid and sterile. The floor, the walls, and even the ceiling, are covered with what appears to be a thin, plastic sheeting. However, it does not feel thin or plastic as I step on it; it feels as though I am stepping on nothing, an absence. That sensation, eerie and indescribable, is soon forgotten as I notice the operating table at the center of the room. I go stiff at the sight of it and my two keepers have to drag me to it.

They force me to sit on its edge, holding me there as I try several times to get up. It is very thin, made from a kind of plastic that is almost translucent, contoured to match the shape of a body. It is designed to be lain upon face down, with restraints ready to be snapped in place over the arms, legs, waist, and neck. There is a crank mechanism at one end, apparently allowing the table to be flipped so that either side of the patient can be accessed with ease.

"Breathe. Slowly," the woman says to me, and I realized that I am hyperventilating, my whole body shaking in terror.

She and the man look on unconcerned as I struggle to regain my equilibrium, their arms crossed over their chests, ready to respond to any aggression on my part in a moment. Behind them is another man, the driver, or the one who caught me in the market, the fourth person not joining us in the room. He busies himself at a nearby counter, which I failed to notice earlier, drawing some fluid into a needle.

"I'll need you to take your clothes off," he says, as he taps at the needle to get an air bubble out. I do not respond, staring straight ahead, hearing the words but not understanding them, a catatonia seizing me.

"Very well," he says, and waves a hand at my two keepers. They take hold of me again, forcing me down on the table. I fight against them, a frenetic energy seizing my body, which still feels numb and distant from my person. They keep me in place as the man injects me, reflexively patting my arm where the needle pierces my skin. I continue to struggle, kicking out blindly, trying to strike one of them, but they avoid my blows with ease until I can feel my body beginning to slow, my control of its functions slipping.

Blackness descends over my eyes, like a blind being drawn across them, and a loud hum rises in my ears. I lose all feeling in my body not long after, though I can still somehow feel the man who holds my arms recoiling from me and hear as he says, "Damn it, he's pissing himself."

I want to laugh, but oblivion seizes me.

11

Awareness returns slowly. I am lying upon the table, my body in restraints. I feel distant from myself, as though I am standing in another room trying to view the scene through a window. Someone is moving around me, passing from the operating table to the counter and back again. An implement of some sort is picked up or set down, and I feel myself wincing in response. I open my eyes, but I still cannot see, and when I attempt to move my body does not respond.

"Did he have any ID on him?" The voice sounds very near, just off to the left of my head. It is a man's voice but I do not recognize the speaker.

"Yes. Joseph Aurellano. I have Aleksandra and Martin looking into it. I doubt they'll find anything. The Order is very thorough about these things."

That voice I do recognize. It belongs to the man who intercepted me in the market. He is standing by the counter doing something with whatever implement he moved earlier. Desperately I try to recall what was lying on the counter when they brought me in, but all I can see is his face looming over me, his eyes on the needle he is inserting into my arm.

"It makes one wonder how we ever found out about him."

"Too good to be true, you think?" the first man says. He moves from the counter to the operating bed, hovering over me.

"Did you see who he was with?" the stranger says. It seems clear that he is in command.

"Not really. A woman. Knowing Molijc, she won't have her own face."

"Does he?"

As he speaks, he gestures toward my prone body. My awareness seems to expand a moment later, though I still can't see and only dimly hear. Yet I can visualize both men studying me from above. The first man, the doctor, I think, is holding something in his hands, though I can't quite make it out. As I watch him, bracing myself for whatever is to come, I become aware of the presence of a third person in the room standing off to the side, near the door. It is a woman and she watches the proceedings with a skeptical eye.

"No," the doctor says. "Near as I can tell he is the man he was when he was born. If anything was done to him, it was by someone far better than me."

"Strange that they would send someone here on their own face."

The doctor grunts, busy with whatever implement he has at hand. I feel something pierce my spine where it meets my buttocks and can feel the doctor's careful, guiding hand pressing it deeper. I scream, no sound emerging except in my mind, where it echoes loudly until the pain drowns out all my senses and I lose consciousness.

The doctor is speaking when I come to. It feels as though only a few seconds have passed, though I have no way of knowing for certain. Time seems as distant and mercurial as my body. He begins to slowly retract whatever penetrated my spine, and the slow burn of agony inflames my thoughts.

"We'll know soon enough," he says. "What do you want done with him in the meantime?"

The other man considers this for a moment. "Let's wait until the results are in before we do anything. You'll have to keep him in here or the Seeker will be on us."

"Yes. I'll just keep him under."

"Good. I'm going to let the others know about our progress. Keep me informed."

A moment later I can hear him entering the code for the door, which opens with a hiss of air. A satisfied beep announces when it has sealed again. The doctor doesn't look up from his task, moving from where I lie to the counter where he busies himself with some equipment. He hums as he works while I try again to move. My body still does not respond, though it aches from whatever was done to me, a throbbing pain that showed no signs of subsiding.

He injects me again, this time in the shoulder, and the void descends for a time. When I emerge from it the doctor is still humming, busy at the counter, though I sense a great deal of time has passed and he has left and returned. He pays no attention to me, not even glancing in my direction, his focus solely on the device on the counter. I can see him more clearly than before, though my eyes still will not open. It is the difference between a dream and waking, though surely this is some manner of dream. I am standing, watching him intently from the far corner of the room.

"How is that possible?" the doctor says to himself, turning to look at me. As he does, my point of view evaporates and I return to the operating table, my vision reduced to intuition and insinuation.

"Who are you?" he says in a wondering tone.

I have two revelations almost simultaneously after his question. The first is that the words he is speaking, as well

as his earlier conversation, have all been in the language
the Seeker whispered his threat in. Yet, somehow, I
understand every word. The second is that the woman
remains in the room—has she been here all this time?—
silent and watchful, awaiting the outcome of whatever tests
the doctor is running. She is the key to my predicament, I
think, though I can't say why I believe that. If I want
answers I will have to find a way to speak with her.

I drift from consciousness without even realizing it,
and when I awake I discover I have been released from the
chair and my clothes returned to me. I am alone in the
room, curled uncomfortably in the corner, as far from the
operating table and counter as possible. The room is dark,
but when I sit up, trying to work the kinks from my neck,
the lights click on. The lower part of my back is still in
agony from the injection I received, pain radiating from it
at the slightest movement.

I ignore it as best I can, forcing myself up onto my
unsteady feet so that I can investigate my surroundings. I
go to the door first, confirming it is locked, and study the
keypad, quickly realizing I have no hope of figuring out the
code. Instead I turn my attention to the counter, where I
see several needles of various sizes and a machine, not
unlike a centrifuge, filled with vials containing fluids of
indeterminate origin. A screen is connected to it, providing
a readout of some sort, but I can make sense of none of
the numbers or measures.

As I squint at the machine, trying to get a better sense
of what it does, the door hisses open and the doctor
enters, along with another man. Though his features are
unfamiliar, I have a very strong sense that this is the
stranger who was present while the doctor performed his
procedure. I am disappointed that the woman is not with
them, for she is the one I want to speak with. The doctor
seals the door and they both approach me warily, unsure
of what to expect.

"Joseph? That is your name?" the stranger says to me, and I nod. "Good. We have some questions for you."

"And why would I answer them?" I say, throwing my head up in what I hope is a gesture of defiance.

"I think you'll find your stay here more pleasant if you do."

I shrug as if I couldn't care less. Unlike the doctor, who is dressed more or less as I am, the stranger wears a powder-blue suit, ostentatious and encumbering, that puts me in mind of a grandee at some eighteenth century court. It appears to me to be a uniform, clearly signaling his position to all who laid eyes on it, though I had no idea what authority it represents. Clearly he expects me to be familiar with it, or him, judging by his manner.

"And what do I call you?" I say.

"My name is not important," he says with a smile.

"Dick it is," I say in reply, surprising myself and him.

"Very funny," he says. "Are we through with the juvenile games?"

"When I am, you'll be the first person I let know, Dick." I have no idea where this bravado is coming from, for I feel none of it.

He looks at me grimly. "I am not a patient man, so I will ask you these questions only once and I expect helpful answers. You are from this universe and you have never left it?"

"To the best of my knowledge," I say with a smile.

The man glances at the doctor, who says, "It's like I said. The results are very clear. His spinal fluid has none of the markers from a crossing."

"What is your involvement in the Church of Regents?" the man says, turning his attention back to me.

"First I've heard of it, Dick," I say.

He smiles thinly. "I find that doubtful, given that we saw you in the company of one of their agents."

"It's the truth. Besides, you don't even know who I was with."

This seems to take him by surprise, and he glances at the doctor, who says, "I saw her in the market."

"Probably," I say, smiling at them both. "But you don't know who she is. Just like you don't know who I am. And I have no idea what you're talking about. I'm clearly not what you expected, so maybe you've got the wrong man."

The man laughs, though there was no mirth in the sound. "Yes, the Seeker just happens to be following the two of you wherever you go. What a marvelous coincidence. Do you really think you are the only ones with Society contacts? We know who has crossed over to this side. We know you tried to cross over there. And you speak the language of the Church. Do you take us for fools? The Grand Regent has badly overestimated us, just as he has greatly overestimated his own importance to the True Faith."

I shrug, looking past the two of them. The situation is growing more absurd by the moment. I am answering the man's questions as truthfully as I can, but my honesty can only sound evasive to them. I am not about to admit that I have no memory of who I am or what happened, though they will get it out of me eventually if they are as willing and persistent as they let on. It all depends on how valuable I am to them. Given there are two groups—that I am aware of—along with whoever Meredith is allied with, who want me in their possession, I decide I am valuable enough they won't try anything too extreme.

"Sounds like just the sort of thing a heretic would say, Dick," I say to him.

I can sense him trying to choke back his fury, but it is not to be contained. "I did not cross over here, at considerable risk to my person and my standing, with the damn Society willing to burn the very ground we stand on, to be insulted by the likes of you. You are exactly what is wrong with the Church. The Grand Regent may only value loyalty and servility, but I work for a higher calling."

He is out of breath as he finishes and he does not wait

for a reply, storming from the room, ordering the doctor to see that I provide some answers as he goes.

As soon as we are alone, the doctor smiles and says, "You should have been more compliant with the High Regent. His methods are far gentler than mine. So let us begin."

12

His name, he tells me, is De Vroes, though I doubt that is the truth. He begins with questions that, when my answers prove unsatisfactory, lead to him calling in his companions from the van. They hold me down on the operating table, strapping me in, while he injects me with a blue serum. I can feel its effects immediately, a tightening of my muscles and a loss of equilibrium, so that at various times I feel as though I am standing and about to fall down, others as though I am floating above the table where I lie. De Vroes peers into my pupils to assure himself the drug is working and proceeds to ask me the same questions again.

I do not know what I say in reply. I babble and mutter, rave like a lunatic, speaking endless untruths. This perplexes De Vroes and the other two to no end. They inject me again, with no change in my answers, and do various readings of my body's responses, which only leaves them more confused. I am as baffled as they are, for I have lost all command of my faculties. My awareness is shuttled aside by another, and I am forced to watch as something within me speaks things that are not in my own thoughts.

De Vroes comes to same conclusion, having exhausted his patience with his questioning. "There are two possibilities," he says to the others. "He is a Dissimulator, or he has been made not to know."

"Why would they strip his mind?" the woman says.

"Intriguing, isn't it?" De Vroes says. "We will find out soon enough."

They all exit the room, leaving me strapped to the operating table, the effects of the drug slowly dissipating, my mind gradually returning to me. As I lie there, trying not to dwell on what might happen to me upon their return, my thoughts turn to my newfound ability to speak this strange language, a language from another universe. I speak it with ease, even my unintelligible ravings have largely been in that unfamiliar tongue, and now I find my thoughts are being formed in it, almost as frequently as they are in English.

Is this, I wonder, a sign that my memory is returning? It seems clear that it must be, yet no other memories come with the return of, what I assume to be, my native tongue. But is it?

De Vroes said I show no sign of having crossed over from whatever universe they come from, but Meredith said we came here together. Who to trust? De Vroes and the Regent Dick were plainly surprised to discover I am native to this world and have no reason I can discern to lie about it, so it seems Meredith has led me astray.

Something was done to me, that much seems clear. My ravings suggest a defense mechanism, put in place to guard whatever lies below it in my mind. Add to that my multiple amnesias and the constant sense I have of dislocation from this body. *It is not my own.* The thought leaves me in despair and I push it aside. Some disconnect was created within me and I have to find out what it is and who has done it. It seems an impossible task.

De Vroes and the two others return while I am in the midst of these thoughts. The woman, who was present during the procedure, and who I am beginning to suspect is a hallucination, is with them as well, though I hardly notice her. My attention is on the black orb that enters with them, floating beside De Vroes, near his shoulder. As it comes closer I see that it is not black, but rather the same deep violet color of the Seeker's eyes, absorbing, not reflecting, the light. The orb is making a sound like a rasping breath being drawn in and out, a being in its last moments. Like myself. I begin to struggle against my bonds.

De Vroes sets up a screen on the counter, angling it so I can't see, and taps away on it, glancing from time to time at the orb. His two assistants set to work on the table, cranking it until it stands almost perpendicular to the floor and the orb descends to my eye level. I turn away from it, wincing at the thing's breathing. Is it somehow alive? The woman gives me a grim smile, as she checks my bonds and tells De Vroes all was ready. The other woman has gone to stand in the corner where I can't see her. I feel her presence behind me, though; it is palpable, her watchful eyes taking in the whole scene, her silence weighing on the shoulders of the three who busy themselves in their preparations.

When everything is set up to De Vroes' satisfaction, he turns his attention to me, standing behind the orb where he has a clear view of the screen, motioning for his assistants to stand on either side of the table. He begins to ask me the same questions as before and I answer them as I did when the Regent Dick was asking them, with a mixture of truth and evasion. I really do know nothing about the Church of the Regent and the Grand Regent, presumably its leader. Nor do I know anything about the Society of Travelers, or Seekers, or any of the rest, beyond what Meredith told me, and I do not trust anything she said.

This time De Vroes pays little mind to what I say. When he asks me, "What is your involvement in the Watchers' Order?" he does not even look at me as I tell him I have never heard of such a thing, his eyes intent on the screen. What do I know of the purge of the High Regents and what was my involvement in it?

"How could I be involved in something over there if I've never left here?" I say to De Vroes, who does not bother to acknowledge my question, continuing to ask me more specifics about the Watchers' Order and whether my attempted return is tied in some way to its machinations.

"What is your purpose here?" he says again, having gone through all the questions he asked before.

"To live and die like anyone else."

He purses his lips as he studies the screen, glancing up at his subordinates to say, "Get Osahi. He will want to see this."

The man leaves and returns a moment later with the Regent Dick, still resplendent in his suit. "What have you found?" he says as he enters the room.

"He's been scraped. He really does remember nothing."

Osahi nods, putting a finger to his chin. "Could it be a tamp?"

"It's possible," De Vroes says. "We'd need to go in. See what we can find."

I look from one man to the other, feeling very much like a frog about to be dissected. They pay no attention to me, Osahi taking a moment to study whatever is on the screen De Vroes set up. I think I can sense the woman behind me, leaning forward from her corner to ensure she does not miss a single nuance of what is said.

"Do it," Osahi says, glancing up from the monitor.

"There's a risk. We may lose him in the procedure."

I feel lightheaded as Osahi considers this. "No. We need to know what he knew and why they tried to bring him over. How soon can you begin?"

"Within the hour."

"Good," Osahi says, turning to leave the room. "Complete the procedure as soon as you can. I fear that we don't have much time."

"You think they will find us? There was only one

woman with him."

"Something went wrong, clearly, but the more time we give them, the more time they will have to counter us. Whatever this man knows, it is important. The Grand Regent will respond with all the resources at his disposal. I do not need to remind you how considerable those are, or how meager our own are."

"No," De Vroes says. "I will start within the hour and we will be done in three, four at the most."

"Good," Osahi says. He punches in the code to open the door and paused for a moment on the threshold.

"I cannot be discovered here or all is lost," he says, looking from face to face in the room before stepping outside, the door hissing shut behind him. There is a long pause as De Vroes and his two assistants stare at the door, the weight of the moment clear on their faces.

De Vroes turns to look at me and says, "Let's begin."

13

I feel adrift, unmoored from all sense of myself, awake one moment and unconscious the next, unable to distinguish between the two. De Vroes appears from time to time to check on my vitals and to administer further drugs, plunging me further into this disorienting sea of darkness. There are storms in the distant murk, filled with vague flashes of light, creeping across the periphery of my vision. The lights are blue and green, edged with hints of gold and violet, shaped into a line of thin circles with frayed edges, that go bright and dim and bright again. They are above and then below, always on the very edge of my vision, no matter how I strain to catch a clear glimpse. Within the circles of light I am certain I can see images and details, but no matter how hard I try they will not come into focus.

I lapse into a deeper reverie, and awake sometime later to find myself alone still strapped to the table. My body aches from being constrained in one position for so long, but it is a dull pain, distant from my other sensations. I cannot seem to feel the table or see the room properly. It is as though I am floating in another dimension only tenuously connected to this one.

The woman stands over me, though I did not notice her enter the room. Perhaps she has been there all along. Her face seems more familiar now. I know that I have seen her somewhere before, though I can't yet place where. The memory is so tantalizingly near I can almost feel it, as if the thought has gained substance. She leans in so that her face almost brushes against mine and I can feel her breath upon my lips, as her eyes seek my depths.

"What do you remember?" she whispers.

It is not a demand, as Osahi and De Vroes' questions were—it is an entreaty, and I feel compelled to answer. I try to summon my thoughts, to command my memories forth from the void where they are imprisoned. The void remains, a place of darkness, empty and showing no signs of anything being hidden there. Just as I begin to despair and to stutter forth a reply to her question, the lights become visible again at the bottom corner of my eye, growing brighter and larger, until they burst forth at the center of my vision, unfurling like a flower going into bloom. They take form and shape and become memories, thoughts, my being, all of myself returning at once in a blinding torrent. It is so fast, such an assault, that I find myself gasping for breath.

"What do you remember?" she says again, putting her hand on mine to calm me.

Everything, I want to say to her, but am unable to. There are multitudes within me, bursting to life, with the promise of more to come, but there is no sense to it, no coherence. An image here, a scrap of conversation there, familiar faces without names. It is all too much, I do not have the means to process it. The woman squeezes my hand and says, "It will come."

"I know who I am," I say, finding my voice at last, for I have seen myself in amidst all the other recollections and at last my self-image has footing.

"Yes," she said. "Who are you?"

"David Aeida," I say with conviction. "I am David

Aeida, sub-Regent of the Watchers' Order."

"It will come," she says, and smiles, releasing my hand. I close my eyes, trembling, tears threatening to burst forth. It feels so good, is a relief beyond measure, to know with a certainty who I am. The feeling of dislocation, of not being myself, of my face and thoughts all being false, is gone, replaced by this sort of jagged madness. But as the woman said, it will come; the pieces will find their proper order.

I try to speak, wanting to express my thanks to her, for helping, even as I wonder why she is and why I trust her so absolutely. *I know her.* That is why, though I cannot recall her name or how our paths crossed. That doesn't explain my trust, though, for she is here, in league with subversives, intent on thwarting the Grand Regent. I wrestle with my mind, trying to find some memory, however slender, that will shed light on this apparent contradiction, but none is forthcoming.

As I open my mouth to speak, she puts a finger to her lips and gives a shake of her head, nodding to the ceiling, suggesting we are being monitored. She leans in close, as though to give me a kiss on the cheek, and whispers in my ear, "Remember."

As she says it, she glances toward the door and then walks over to it. My eyes follow her and I watch as she steps aside, giving me a clear view of the keypad, and types in the code. The door hisses open and she walks out, at the same time as De Vroes walks in, the two of them sharing a barely acknowledged glance. De Vroes turns and watches the door shut, ensuring that it is locked, wanting to be certain she is gone before proceeding.

"You're awake, I see," he says.

I try to speak, but my mouth is dry and my tongue heavy, leaving my words slurred and garbled. De Vroes pays no attention to me, turning to the counter, filling a needle with another of his elixirs. He peers into my eyes as he injects me and says, as I begin to blink and drift into that unsteady darkness, "What do you remember?"

14

When I awake next the restraints are gone from my arms and legs. I try to get up from the operating table and nearly fall to the floor. Two sets of strong hands seize me by the shoulders and drag me to a chair someone has brought into the room. I slump into it, my legs jutting out in odd directions. My body feels leaden, my mind dull and vague, and I briefly wonder if I am still asleep, but dismiss the idea out of hand. This is no dream.

Two other chairs are brought into the room and De Vroes and Osahi sit across from me, their faces grim and strained. Their assistants, the man and the woman, stand on either side of me, ready to act should I attempt anything, though it is clear I am in no shape to do any such thing. The woman is absent, I am certain, though I was unable to get a good look at the rest of the room, as they transferred me to the chair. Now I try to focus on De Vroes and Osahi, but my eyes keep wandering and I find myself staring at nothing, my vision a blur.

"Let's begin," Osahi says. He has taken off his suit jacket, I see, revealing a finely tailored white shirt, with emerald buttons that gleam. I become entranced by their color, seeing in them the same line of lights that presaged the return of my self.

Before he can utter another word, I announce to the room, in a voice heavy with sleep or drugs, "I am David Aeida, sub-Regent of the One True Church, and you are holding me against my will."

Osahi raises an eyebrow. "Well, now. Do you know who I am, David Aeida?"

I stare at him, confused by the question. I know him. He is Osahi, the Regent Dick. I want to say that to him, but the words are choked in my throat.

"I am Toma Osahi, High Regent of the One True Church. You, sub-Regent, are under my command, and you will remain here until you answer any questions I may have, to my satisfaction. Do you understand?"

"You are acting in contravention of the protocols of the Church, and I will not answer to you," I try to say, but my reply is a stream of garbled, stuttered nonsense.

Osahi shares a glance with De Vroes, who leans forward and says, "Tell us what you remember, David. You are not well. We might be able to help you."

That is lie. I am just suffering from the aftereffects of the drugs they administered and the procedure they performed on me. I know who I am with clarity and certainty. I am David Aeida, sub-Regent of the Watchers' Order. I cling to that singular thought through the buzzing of so many conflicting others that threaten to overwhelm me.

"How were you recruited into the Watchers' Order?" Osahi says bluntly, dispensing with any pretense.

I stutter something out, not even sure myself of what I am saying. The High Regent frowned, leaning back in his chair to stroke his chin. I recognize him now: Toma Osahi, High Regent, one of five who administer particular sections of the Church beneath the Grand Regent. Osahi is in charge of the Regents in the Church's home universe, so I know he is operating well beyond his jurisdiction here. I have no need to answer to him. The Watchers' Order answers only to the Grand Regent. Not that I am at all capable of answering, even if I wanted to.

"What were your responsibilities on this world? Why did you attempt to cross over into ours? What was your purpose?" These questions come from Osahi in staccato bursts, his frustration apparent.

I blink at him and look at myself, becoming aware for the first time that I am dressed again. I can see my jacket lying on the counter and I find myself wondering if my phone is still in it.

"Your buttons are not the light. The light is in me. It is me. When I see it I will be whole," I say. "This is not the impossible world. It is out there to be found."

Osahi raises an eyebrow at my ravings and turns to De Vroes. "How long will it take for him to stabilize?"

The other shrugs. "He may not. Even if he does, it may take days until we know for certain."

"We don't have days," Osahi says, biting off the words.

"I know. This was always this risk with the procedure. But he definitely remembers, that much seems certain. I think if we keep at it we may learn something."

Osahi nods and turns his attention to me. "There is no point in trying to hide anything from us. We will find it out given time, and I will ensure that we have it. Now tell me, what was your purpose in the Order?"

I shudder at his words. One of the lights, still hovering, just visible, near the edge of my vision, bursts into fluorescence. I see, in an instant, an entire audience with the Grand Regent. I kneel before him, receiving his blessing and welcome to the Holy Order. He has a special mission for me, he says, one of utmost delicacy, which will require the ultimate sacrifice. *I am a regent for my true body*, I tell him. *You may do with this flesh as you must.*

He thanks me and we are joined by two of his attendants, people I do not recognize, but whom I instinctively know are Acolytes like De Vroes. I follow them to an operating table. Strangely, my perspective on these events is not my own; it comes from a place near the operating table, shrouded in darkness. There is something there, almost visible, but I cannot bear to look.

Is this dream or memory? As I ask the question, I snap back into awareness and see Osahi and De Vroes staring intently at me.

"What do you remember?"

I am given no chance to answer the question, for an alarm begins to shriek, echoing throughout the building.

Osahi leaps from his chair, his face gone white, sweat forming on his upper lip. "The Seeker," he says, to no in particular. His words seem to paralyze the others and they all stand looking up at the ceiling, as though it might reveal the proper course of action.

"We have to get you out of here," De Vroes says, breaking the reverie.

"There's no time," Osahi says, his composure returning with a shake of his head. "We'll have to make a stand here." He turns to me. "How many men were with him?"

When I do not answer immediately he grows furious, stomping across the room to loom over where I slump in the chair. "Answer me. Your life is forfeit here as well. How many men were there?"

"Two," I manage to say, my voice the barest of whispers.

Osahi nods, his eyes distant, as though he is performing some sort of calculation. "Come on," he says, heading for the door and punching in the code. De Vroes follows on his heels and the two assistants grasp me by the shoulders to carry me out.

"Leave him," De Vroes says. "He's not going anywhere, and the Seeker may not know he's here yet."

They drop me back onto the chair and hurry after Osahi and De Vroes, sealing the door behind them. The pulse of the alarm seems to recede, though I know the volume has not changed. I am simply less present, my jumbled thoughts and memories surging over my consciousness again. I seem to be both floating and sinking into the chair simultaneously, inhabiting two distinct states of being in the same instant.

The panic I know I should be feeling at the news that the Seeker is here fails to materialize. It seems a distant concern, as opposed to a particularly sharp memory of a sunlit walk down East Main Street toward downtown. I pass by a small bar called the Whip and, at a whim, stop to have a beer. I sit on the patio watching the passersby, the girls in sun dresses, the hours slipping away.

The cessation of the alarm, and the ominous silence that follows, return me to my present self, and I realize that I need to escape this room, that now is my opportunity. It surprises me that they left me unattended. The Seeker has to be here for me, after all, in spite of what De Vroes said.

This room, though...I remember something about this room. The plastic sheeting walls and ceiling and floors, they are shields against the Seeker. He can't track me so long as I remain here, but that matters little now that he has found this building. Eventually he and the Black Robes will find their way into this room. And if they do not, well, it's not as though I want to remain the prisoner of the High Regent.

I try to force myself to stand up, to no avail; my body will not respond. It seems to take a force of will just to blink or breathe. What did they do to me?

Outside the door I can hear loud voices, sounding dim through the walls, and I cease all my attempts to get up, my face going flush at the thought of being discovered trying to flee. Perhaps it is better to remain where I am for the moment, I tell myself. But the woman showed me the code. My thoughts are sluggish, piecing things together in agonizing slow motion. This might be the distraction she intended me to take advantage of.

As my mind wars at itself, one thought compelling me

to rise, the next to remain inert, further shouts and some muffled crashes reach my ears. The origin of these noises is unclear to me, but I think it unlikely that it is coming from directly outside the door. I imagine a battle between Osahi, and his followers, and the Seeker, and his black-robed minions, taking place from room to room above me, until one side lies vanquished, their blood staining the floors. I wonder what weapons they might be using and cannot remember. Swords? Revolvers? There is a blank where the thought should be.

The gap troubles me for some reason and, as I worry at it, another flash of memory blinds me. I see myself walking down a narrow corridor, one I have traversed endless times. The building it is located in won't come to me, but I know it is a massive and forbidding structure. Why I am there and where I am going—those details are absent, all context stripped from the memory, leaving only this precious shard. The smell of the place, a hint of lavender and ostentation, is heavy on my nostrils now. The feel of the carpet beneath my feet and the cool recycled air are palpable to me, left here in this hot, miserable place.

As I walk down the corridor I encounter someone—a woman, whose face is obscured somehow. I blink, trying to bring her into focus, to no avail. We embrace, a lover's embrace, passion and desire coursing through me. But not her. I can feel her distance from me, and I understand—this is the exact moment of my revelation—that she will betray me. As we disentangle from each other's arms, I look into her eyes to see if her treachery is visible there. But her face is emotionless, masked with an expression I know only too well, for the obscurity of memory has dissolved, and it is Meredith staring back at me.

15

I am still disoriented by the cascades of memories assaulting me, trying desperately to cling to this latest revelation that sprung forth, only to disappear into the ether, when a scream interrupts my thoughts. All my questions, whether Meredith and I were lovers, the nature of her betrayal, and how I can have been in the other universe—for there seems no doubt the corridor where we met is not located in this world—dissolve at the sound. Another scream follows—a woman's voice—and I know, with a terrible certainty, that I have to escape now or my life will be forfeit.

I summon my remaining will, trying to push aside the constant buzzing of my thoughts, the lights ebbing and flowing like the tide in the corner of my eyes, and clamber to my feet. I stand above the chair for a moment, unsteady and feeling ill, before picking up my jacket and putting it on. The concentration and effort it takes to manage that small task is exhausting.

I try to ignore that feeling and take a lurching step toward the keypad. It seems to take hours for me to cross the room to the door, each step a monumental effort from which I have to recover. My body still feels weighted by some obscene gravity—was I transported somehow to another planet, I wonder—and my thoughts won't go quiet, leaving me to gather and orient myself from moment to moment.

Something like the aftershock of an explosion shakes the room, sending me tumbling to floor. I lie there cringing, waiting for the next rumble to overtake me. When none comes, I regain my footing and go to the keypad, a burst of adrenaline washing away the numbness from my body, and enter in the code the woman showed me. After a sickening pause, where I am certain I was fooled, or simply dreamed it all wholesale, the door hisses open and I step out into the hallway.

It is empty and exactly as it was when the High Regent's people brought me here. There is no sign of the pitched battle that I imagine must be occurring between the Seeker and the High Regent. I close the door to my prison and stand listening, trying to gauge where everyone is and if there is anyone nearby. The corridor is quiet and dim; the building seems to have gone absolutely still. I think I can hear the traffic passing by outside on whatever street is nearest.

I try to retrace my steps, though my recollection of that afternoon is clouded by all my new emerging memories, to the back alley, where I am certain the van will still be. I can use it to escape, although I am not sure I can trust myself to walk, let alone drive. Though my thoughts are still confused, unbidden memories paralyzing me at any given moment, my footsteps are steadier with each stride and my confidence in my chances of making good my escape soar.

My growing euphoria lasts until I come to the first intersection and make to turn down a hallway I am certain leads to the back of the building. There I run square into one of the Black Robes as he strides down the corridor. The force of our collision sends me to the ground, scrambling frantically away from him. He grunts in surprise and bends over to seize me by the collar of my shirt and, without breaking stride, drags me stumbling along behind him. Surprising myself, I curse him and my misfortune, and he glances down at me and laughs.

He leads me to a room near the front of the building, where a wall pockmarked with empty window frames gives me a view of the foyer and the street outside. The sun is bright and I can almost smell the glory of summer and idleness that lies beyond. Such a life is not given to me, though. The Black Robe throws me at the feet of Seeker, who is crouched peering around a doorway from which I can see a corridor leading to a set of stairs.

"I have found the transgressor," the Black Robe says, surprising me by speaking in English.

"Yes." The Seeker does not even glance at me, his alien eyes intent upon the corridor. "I fear they have killed Asdrubal."

"Let us see them answer for it."

The Seeker holds up a hand. "Patience. They have an unbinder."

The word sends chills through me, for I now know the portent of doom they hold. The Seeker and the Black Robe appear unconcerned for the moment. They would be; it is their nature to believe themselves impervious to harm.

The crimes the High Regent has committed here are beyond measure, I realize in a sudden insight. Not only has he transported himself and these others across the universes, he brought a quantum weapon with him. We lesser mortals are not to possess such weapons, just as we are not to cross over, and to commit both acts at once is so unforgivable the Society will work to ensure an example is made of them.

Why take such a risk? For me, I realize, it is all for me. But what knowledge do I possess that can justify such an undertaking? I search my mind, my fragmented and chaotic memories, and find nothing that can shed light on that. All I see within is madness, barely contained, threatening to breach the dike of my carefully constructed being and overwhelm me.

The Seeker motions for the Black Robe to take his place at the doorway and turns his empty gaze upon me. I flinch at his stare, wanting to turn away, but somehow am compelled to meet his eyes. They seem to hold infinities.

"So you are with the Regent cult," he says. His voice has traces of an accent I cannot place. South African, perhaps? "I did not know their infection had spread to this universe as well. What pitiful life did you lead here to cause you to fall sway to their fantasies?"

I swallow. I do not know what to say but his eyes, his very being, seem to compel an answer. "I do not remember."

"Curious," he says, looking me up and down, as though he misjudged me and wonders how. "Curious. Why did you try to cross over?"

"I do not remember," I say. Flashes of memories blur past, and I try to cling to the images, the scents, the words, but they all disintegrate at my touch. "They tried to get my memory back."

"When time allows we will see what we can do on that front," the Seeker says. I find no comfort in the offer. "For now we will deal with your compatriots. Any attempt to stop us would be unwise."

I nod, not bothering to tell him that, given I can hardly walk, I am not going to be thwarting anything.

The Seeker turns to the Black Robe and says, "Do you see anything?"

The Black Robe glances back and shakes his head. As he does, something like a beam of light captured him and his body goes rigid, his face contorting in agony. Moving faster than I ever imagined possible, the Seeker leaps to the Black Robe and knocks him free of the beam, passing through it himself as he does. Both of them are left writhing on the floor in agony, their mouths open as if to scream or cry, but no sound comes forth.

I stare at them in horror, wondering if these are perhaps their death throes. From the stairs above I hear a cry of triumph, cut short by a curt order from Osahi. I wait, but no other sound emerges. It seems no one is willing to venture below to see if they have, in fact, delivered a killing blow, though the Seeker and the Black Robe remain contorted on the floor. Their convulsions gradually dissipate and the Seeker manages to raise himself to his elbows and looks up the stairs, which are still empty, before turning his gaze to me.

His visage is contorted by the agonies he is suffering, yet somehow remains without emotion, a terrifying combination, and I shiver to witness it. The beam, still visible, transforming the air it touches, divides the room, placing me on one side and him on the other, and our eyes link through the shimmering air. He seems unable, for the moment, to do anything, and I, sensing my chance, get to my feet and make my way to one of the empty window frames, beyond which lies the foyer and freedom.

His eyes seem to bore into me, though I can detect no change in their opaque lenses, commanding me to remain where I am. I find myself torn between competing compulsions: the need to obey the Seeker, and the sure knowledge that to remain here a moment longer will be to imperil myself. In the end it is the woman who decides it for me. The memory of her whispered encouragement propels me forward. I have no idea if it was her scream I heard earlier, but I do not want her gift to be in vain. If it is important to her that I escape, then it is important to me.

As the Seeker watches, unmoving, I clamber through the window frame and make my way through the foyer and out to the street and the welcome glare of the sun. I breathe deep of the fresh air, luxuriating in the sensation of being outside. Parked on the street is the silver car I am certain the Seeker and the Black Robes were driving when they found Meredith and me in the apartment building. I walk around to the driver's side and find the door unlocked and slip inside.

From outside the car looked like any other, but within the dashboard is unlike any I have seen, filled with gauges and screens I can make no sense of. There is no ignition, only a series of buttons where the stereo and dials for the heat and air conditioning would be. I press one, trusting my instinct, and the car starts, ghostly silent, the engine barely humming. I pull into traffic and drive away.

16

The whir of the engine, so slight I have to strain to hear it over the sound of the other cars on the road, is a comfort as I flee. It feels familiar, a sound that formed the background to a thousand memories, and seems to quiet the cacophony of my thoughts, filled with memories that jabber and caper about, each demanding my attention. The contradiction inherent in the comfort—how can this car, with its engine from another universe, be familiar to me?—is something I can ignore while it eases my anguish. But for how long? That thought too is there, lurking beneath these spiraling recollections, these multitudes I suddenly contain that seem to be fighting to burst free.

I am David Aeida, I tell myself, repeating it like an invocation. All of the rest, my garbled memories, the absent knowledge that the High Regent and even the Seeker believes I possess, will sort itself out given time. Didn't the woman tell me it will come with time? Meredith did as well. The memory of her false embrace arises in my mind, demanding my attention, though I try not to think of it, to not replay the moment again and again. Though the memory has no context, it feels like an open wound each time I return to it, and yet I am compelled to.

Can I trust her now? Who else do I have to trust? She is of the Order, as am I, and, in spite of the embrace, she is the only thing resembling an ally I have.

It takes me some time to determine where I am as I drive, but eventually, as I follow the flow of the traffic, I spot the ocean gleaming in the sunlight and the bridge spanning the bay leading back to downtown. There are mountains behind me to the north and at last I recognize where I am. Vancouver. The Lions Gate Bridge. After the bridge comes Stanley Park, a forested peninsula spidered with paths, all of which give the appearance of leading deep into some world apart.

I pull off onto some street in the west end of downtown just on the park's edge, leaving the car there and returning to the park on foot. Before I leave it I do a quick search to see if there is anything of use. In the glove box I find what, at a glance, appears to be a flashlight, though its weight and the feel of the material tells me otherwise. There is a small, thin button along one side of its length that can be depressed to activate the device, though I do no such thing, not wanting to attract any attention. The center console holds a tiny box, no bigger than a wallet, with a few wires extending from it. It looks as though it is a very small voltage meter, or something of this sort, though the box itself has no gauges, or even a switch or button that suggests how it works.

I study both tools carefully, unsure of what they are, hoping to spark some memory. When none comes I slip them both in my jacket pockets, thinking that I will ask Meredith what they are when I find her. The thought surprises me, nearly causing me to stop in the middle of the street as I walk away from the car. Is that my plan? Find Meredith. I remember her words to me the day this madness started: *friends of convenience*. Now memory tells me otherwise.

I push those tangled thoughts from my mind as best I can and make my way to the beach where the sea wall path that wraps around Stanley Park begins. It is filled with people out for a stroll or a jog. I hear at least a half-dozen different languages spoken, the strange voices and phrases seeming to mimic the babble of my own thoughts. The sun and the sea air restores me, at least physically, each step no longer an effort requiring concentration. I begin to feel more of myself.

After half an hour or so I begin to feel hungry and dizzy, so I find a bench and sit down, watching the passersby and, beyond them, the waves crashing against the sea wall. The rhythm of the sea, the pulse of earth, lull me and I find myself drifting into sleep and have to shake myself awake. I cannot let my guard down, even in this idyllic place. No one followed me from the building as best I can see, but there is no telling how long the confrontation between the Seeker and the High Regent will last and who will emerge triumphant. Whoever did, they will certainly come looking for me. And I know of nowhere to hide.

That last fact tells me why I have to find Meredith, even if I can't trust her. So long as I am compromised, filled with these disordered half-memories, there is no chance I can fend for myself against the likes of the Seeker or the High Regent. I need her, as terrible as it is to admit it. Worst of all, I have no idea how to find her in this vast city.

As I mull these thoughts, the memories that have continued to bubble beneath the surface of my consciousness, evaporate and the void descends upon me. The terrible silence that follows, the ache left by the absence I can almost trace in my mind, lands like a blow. I have to stop myself from crying out, from rising to my feet in panic.

The woman's face returns to me, calm and gentle, and I can feel her hand upon my arm as she whispers to me, "Remember. It will come."

I am David Aeida, I tell myself, trying to breathe, trying to stop my hands from shaking. *I am David Aeida.* It no longer feels true.

As I try to contain my panic, to stop myself from shaking, or crying aloud, or worse, a voice from on the pathway calls out.

"Hello, David."

I look up, terror wrenching my stomach, and see Meredith looking at me, waiting for me to say something. When I do not reply, she walks over and sits beside me on the bench, neither of us looking at the other, our eyes instead on the sea as it crests upon the land.

THREE:

THE WATCHERS' COMPOUND

17

It is Meredith who breaks the silence. "We can't stay here long. They'll be after us soon. They'll find the car and they'll come here."

I swallow, the emotion and desperation I feel threatening to break loose. "How did you find me?"

"I followed the Seeker," she says with a smile. "Once I lost you, I knew he would still be looking for you. So I waited. It took him quite a while, I have to say."

My fingers are numb and I clench and unclench my hands, trying to return the feeling to them. "They had me in a room. It had some...I don't know, plastic on the walls."

"A sightless room. Clever," Meredith says. We are speaking in English, I note, though still in a low tone in case anyone should overhear us. "I'm surprised they were so well prepared. I may have to revise my estimation of the High Regent. Not that it matters."

I turn to look at her. She is staring into the distance, her head angled so that she can look at me from the corner of her eyes, a sardonic smile tugging at her lips.

"You lied to me," I say.

She goes very still, the edges of her smile just beginning

to fade. "What do you mean?" she says, her voice so quiet I could barely hear it.

"You said there was a war with the Society of Travelers. That we were exiles. You told me nothing about the Church or the Watchers' Order, which apparently I'm a member of. And if we can't travel to the other worlds, we're apparently the only ones."

"I'm sorry. You were confused enough I didn't want to make the situation any worse, especially not with the Seeker so near. And there was some truth in it. We are in a war with the Travelers. They think they are gatekeepers for all the universes. For now they are, but it will not always be so."

She falls silent, considering her words. "But we are exiles here, make no mistake. Crossing over, even communicating, is difficult. The High Regent was a fool for coming; his life is now forfeit."

"You think the Seeker will defeat them? They have an unbinding weapon."

She waves a hand. "It will make no difference. Not against the Seeker. That is why we have to leave now, while we still have time."

I frown and shake my head. "No. Not until you tell me who I am and why everyone is after me."

"We don't have time for this," Meredith says, drawing a glance from a couple as they ran past, dressed in matching track suits.

"Make time," I say, watching the couple disappear around the bend. "How do I know that I wouldn't be better off with the Seeker than you? I know I'm not from over there, I'm from this world, and my memories were taken from me. How do I know it wasn't you who did it?"

"We did do it," she says, squeezing my shoulder, her face a picture of concern. "We did it and you agreed to it. The Grand Regent asked you to make this sacrifice because what you knew was too important for others to find out, and we knew they would be coming."

"Why? Why would the Seeker come after me? I'm from this world. I've never crossed over."

Meredith stands up, casting her eyes down the sea wall pathway. "I will answer any of your questions as best I can. I will not hide anything from you, but we have to go now. The Seeker is coming. You are not safe with him."

The fear in her voice and on her face is real, there is no disguising that. Having been face to face with the man only a few short hours before, I understand only too well what terrifies her. The question is whether I will be any safer in her hands. Only time will tell. I stand up and see relief wash over her face.

Meredith takes me by the hand and leads me along the sea wall path, setting a hard pace. At the first point where the trail branches off we follow it, heading deeper into the park, the massive trees looming above us, casting us in their shadows. There are only a handful of people on the trail, all speaking in low tones, as though they are afraid to disturb the placid silence that reigns in the forest. Meredith takes out her cell phone and calls someone, telling them to meet us along the road near the aquarium. She quickens her pace again and I am soon out of breath. We emerge from the forest onto one of the side roads that bisect the park and start along it, until a car pulls up alongside us.

"Get in," Meredith says, motioning me to the back. "And don't say anything. The driver doesn't know who you are, and the less he knows the better."

I do as she says, sliding into the back seat as she gets in beside the driver, trying to ignore my growing disquiet. I have committed myself to this path, I tell myself, and I will just have to see where it leads. The driver glances in the mirror once as I settle myself, our eyes meeting briefly, before turning his attention to the road. I do not recognize him, nor does he seem to know me.

"You weren't followed?" Meredith says, as the car merges into traffic, heading north back toward the Lions Gate Bridge.

"No. Best I could tell there was no one tailing you either."

Meredith nods. "Good. Take us to the house."

The rest of our journey passes in silence, the driver keeping his eyes on the road ahead, while Meredith keeps watch behind to see who might be following. I try to look out the window at the passing landscape—the bridge and harbor below, a tree-lined freeway, followed by the banality of suburbia—but the undercurrent of tension I can feel from both Meredith and the driver distracts me, and has me glancing behind to see if the Seeker is in pursuit. There are no signs that I can see, and soon we found ourselves in an affluent suburb on a road that winds its way up the side of a mountain, with exits into increasingly more opulent neighborhoods.

As we go I take stock of myself and the situation I find myself in. The returned memories, the relentless, disorienting flood, so terrifying to experience, are still gone, and I feel their absence more keenly than before, having tasted them. I can remember all that has happened to me since the afternoon in the park with a piercing clarity, as well as those memories that somehow broke through the surface of my consciousness after De Vroes' procedure: my audience with the Grand Regent and Meredith's embrace. That I remember these events, but have lost the rest, leaves me oddly hopeful. If these memories remain, perhaps the others will return given time. Again I recall the woman's words to me in the sightless room: *It will come.*

In the meantime, I have to find a way to survive in the vipers' nest I find myself in. It seems that everyone wants what was in my head, either to possess it for themselves, or to ensure that no one else can. Here I can use my fragmented mind to my advantage, for Meredith has no way of knowing what I remember and what I don't, nor what I discovered while the prisoner of the High Regent. No matter what, I cannot forget who I am. I must cling to that at all costs. *I am David Aeida.*

Our journey ends atop the mountain, along a winding road populated with enormous mansions looking down upon the vast city below. The harbor and downtown are visible, the sea awash in the sun, a glorious blue, even at this distance. It is a breathtaking view, which I give but a glance, my eyes on the house we are arriving at. Built into the side of the mountain, it is three stories tall, with the third floor level with the road. A long bay of windows grants an ample look at the exquisite surroundings. Enclosed by an iron gate, it is a fantastical place. I feel as though I am entering a secret fortress, guarding an unreal world.

The driver watches from his car as Meredith and I walk toward the entrance. As we pass within, I realize that it is not just a fortress to keep the Seeker out, but a prison to keep me inside, and I have to resist a shudder.

18

"I told you I would answer any questions you had," Meredith says. "Now is your chance."

We are sitting across from each other at a long table in the kitchen, on the main floor of the house, finishing the last of a meal of leftover Chinese food. Just below where we sit is a vast living room, filled with expensive furniture, all arranged to grant a clear view of the bay windows that look down the mountain to the sea. The raised kitchen also offers the same view, and I find myself continually drawn to it. An afternoon storm engulfed the mountain as we arrived, obscuring the house in cloud and rain, leaving me with the distinct feeling that we are floating above the earth.

Still marveling at my new surroundings, I say, "Why didn't we come here first?"

Meredith smiles. She looks more at ease than I have ever seen her. "You like it? I was worried about leading them here. This place is too important for us to lose."

"So there was a plan. We weren't just running."

Meredith laughs. "In spite of all appearances, yes. I'm sorry I had to be so..." She hesitates, searching for the right word. "Deceptive. I know you didn't trust me, but I just couldn't be sure what your mental state was, or how you were handling things."

She pauses and looks out the rain-streaked window. "The man we were supposed to meet at the market was going to give me a stealth mechanism, so that we could get around without worrying about the Seeker."

"Better than the buttons?"

"Yes. They create a kind of pocket universe, a half-world, part of this one, but not. It's enough to hide you from someone like the Seeker, provided you stay still. But you can't stay in them long—the cold you felt is not a good thing—and once he suspected that we were using them, they would have brought equipment to detect them. Which is why I left them in the apartment building for them to find. Bought us a little time. This thing we have now masks us, like this house, or the room you were in with the High Regent."

"You weren't expecting the Seeker then?"

"No, not so soon." She makes a face and hesitates, deciding whether to say more. "We tried to cross you over and there were problems."

"Why cross me over?"

Meredith sighs and pushes her plate away, getting up to put on a kettle. She sets out two cups and puts some tea in a pot, before turning back to me.

"It was getting dangerous here. With what you...had discovered. The Order knew you couldn't remain here, we had to get you to my world, where the Grand Regent could protect you. But we were betrayed, by someone within the Church. Maybe by Osahi, but I don't think so," she says, in answer to my unasked question.

"They stopped you from crossing over," she continues, "so we had to make a decision as to what to do. The Grand Regent decided we couldn't risk your knowledge falling into the wrong hands, and so he asked you to make the sacrifice that you did. We put a tamp in your brain and sealed off your memories."

I consider what she said as the kettle begins to boil and she prepares the tea. It matches what De Vroes said, that my mind was scraped, my memories tamped. Presumably they removed the tamp, letting loose the memories. Why, then, had they disappeared again? I have no explanation and I do not want to ask Meredith for one. It appears she doesn't realize that the tamp was removed and my memories returned, however briefly. Best to keep her in the dark, I reason, gain what knowledge I can from her, while I wait for the memories to resurface.

"Why did I have trouble crossing over?" I ask her. "It doesn't seem anyone else does."

Meredith smiles, putting milk in her tea. She is open and generous today, such a different person than the one I met before. What has changed? She has me fully under her command now, the threat from the Seeker distant, at least for the moment.

"Don't be fooled," she says. "You've just about met the sum total of everyone who has every crossed over to this universe. For the Society, it's easy. They have the knowledge and the technology. For the rest of us, it's trickier, and much more dangerous. We have to cross over in such a way that we don't alert the Society to our having done so. We can't go through the regular gateways, so to speak—we have to go under the wall, or over the fence, and do it without anyone noticing.

"Here's the thing about the universes," she continues, warming to her subject. "They're infinite, right, all independent of each other, functioning by their own laws. To go between them, though, you have to connect them. You're removing something from one and putting it in another, right. That leaves an imprint in both places. You know thermodynamics: every action has an equal and opposite reaction. Same idea, in a way. So it isn't just a matter of connecting the universes and walking through, you have to balance things in each to disguise your coming and going."

"So what happened?" I say.

"Like I said, we were betrayed. Everything was right here to send you over, but over there someone betrayed us. There was no counterbalance in place, no disguise. You would have stepped into the other world and the Society and everyone else would have known."

I rub a hand through my hair and experience a momentary shock. It is close-cropped, almost a buzz cut. I expected it to be longer. I remember the mirror, and my false face within it, and have to suppress a shudder, hoping that Meredith doesn't notice my discomfort.

"And that was eight months ago," I say, remembering what she told me about my memory loss.

"That's right," she says. "We didn't send you through and we put the tamp in your head, because we knew eventually they would track down what universe we were in, no matter what we did, and we couldn't be sure we could keep you safe."

"Shouldn't I remember the last eight months, then?" I say, unable to hide my frustration. The creeping sensation that something is wrong with this body and with my being in it, which subsided with the return of my memories, has reappeared. I have to resist clawing at my flesh, even as I sit here. A side effect of the memory loss, perhaps? Or is it something else? Meredith looks at me, a small frown touching her eyes, and I wonder if my internal struggles are writ large on my face.

"You should. A tamp doesn't stop you from gaining new memories, it just keeps the old ones blocked away. The problem is that we had to block so much of who you were, just to make sure that your knowledge wasn't accessible, that there wasn't much of you left. So the Acolytes decided to give you something of a life, memories, that sort of thing. A transplant personality. But you rejected it, more than once in fact, and when it was gone there was nothing left. It was like you had amnesia."

Meredith's description of what was done to me makes

me want to shudder, but I resist the urge. It also leads to the question: do they want to reconstruct the transplanted personality in me again, to tamp down my memories? The thought repulses me. *It will come.* I get up and walked down the short flight of steps to the living room, trying to hide the strength of the emotion I am feeling. I go to stand before the long windows, gazing down through the mist at the vanishing mountainside.

"Incredible, isn't it," Meredith says, coming to join me. "It should make the days pass easier."

"We'll be here awhile?" I say, fighting to keep my voice even.

"No choice," she says. "Not while the Seeker is still out there. If you stay here, we know he won't be able to find you. We're working on getting him out of the way."

"Killing him?"

"No," Meredith says with a laugh. "I don't know if we could, even if we wanted to. Killing him makes no sense, though. We'd have a half-dozen Seekers from the Guild here looking for vengeance, to say nothing of what the Travelers would do. No, we just need to send him on a false trail, hopefully to another universe. But that will take some doing."

"So I should make myself comfortable," I say.

She ignores or is oblivious to the undercurrent in my voice. "Not to worry, we'll see that you are. Come on, I'll show you your room."

19

The Order's compound, for that is apparently in whose keeping I now am, proves larger even than it appeared from outside. The second and third floors extend deep into the mountain's core—how far I cannot say, for I am not given access to them, except in the most cursory sense. The bedroom Meredith gave me is on the main floor, which I have the run of, and Meredith has shown me a few of the rooms on the floors below, but asked me to stay above at least for the time being.

"Some of the Order are working below," she explains, "and it's better if they don't know who you are or why you're here.

"I don't know which of them I can trust after what happened before," she says, when I am not able to hide the misgivings I feel. "And some of them, like our driver for example, are out in the world every day. I want to make sure they can't reveal anything about you, in case the Seeker or someone else happens upon them."

It all sounds reasonable, and yet the end result is to keep me in a well-contained area where my actions can be easily monitored. That, I am certain, is no coincidence. I offer no complaint, however, appearing to meekly accept the arrangement and to be grateful for all they are providing me. In truth, it is a relief that I do not have to live in immediate fear of the Seeker happening upon me, or De Vroes or someone else interrogating me. There remains a level of tension and anxiety that never leaves me, both at my own growing sense of disorientation with myself, following the loss again of my memory, and the definite feeling I have that this calm is but a prelude to whatever calamity still awaits me.

I give voice to none of this, though I worry all my thoughts are visible upon my face for Meredith to see. If she notices she says nothing, spending her time making a great show of concern for me and all I suffered under the ministrations of the High Regent. Several times she tries to ask me about what befell me, but I feign anguish at recalling it, and she retreats quickly, encouraging me to relax and not dwell on all that has taken place.

"It has been a trying few days," she says, "I can only imagine. If there's anything I can do, please let me know."

Her voice is filled with emotion I can't quite place as she says it, concern etched upon her face as I return her gaze, trying to hide my discomfort. I am left confused, for it seems every time we speak I encounter a new person. One moment she is evasive, demanding obedience, the next conciliatory, full with emotion and sympathy. It only serves to heighten the mistrust I feel for her and increase the sense of doom that shadows the edges of my thoughts, threatening at any moment to consume them entirely with despair.

In the days that follow, I try to distract myself from this gloom by learning as much as I can about the Church and the Watchers' Order, whose members work unseen beneath me. According to Meredith, all of them are, like me, native to this universe and have been recruited by the Order. She is vague on the specifics of their work here, and on the work of the Order in general, as well as why a church needs a compound like this stationed in another universe.

"We have recruits in many universes," she says. "It's the nature of the Church. We believe that, while there are many universes, the multiverse as people call it here, there exists somewhere one true universe, of which all these others are reflections. There resides our true selves; we are but regents. That is why we are here and elsewhere, trying to find the one universe, to be able to unite with our true selves.

"And it is why the Society opposes all we do. They are not believers as we are. They are materialists. Each universe they see as its own creation, not a reflection. It is more complicated, of course, but that is the fundamental of it. They are opposed to any but themselves crossing over and we, naturally, must cross to other universes to find the true one."

"How do you find the true one if there are an infinite number?" I say. We are sitting in main room again, looking out the windows down upon the mountain. It is another rain-filled day, as so many of them have been, the clouds low, mist and fog swirling around.

Meredith smiles. "That is a matter of faith. We believe it is our destiny, and so it will come to pass. The Society thinks us fools. Or worse."

It all seems madness to me, the very existence of the Church and the Society, let alone what each believes. My doubt must be visible on my face, for Meredith smiles and places a hand on my shoulder.

"You doubt everything. It is the same every time. It's too much to absorb at once, I know, especially when it feels like your mind is not your own. And it must feel impossible to know who to trust. We have time now, I hope, for you to sort things out. I want to help you, any way I can."

She leans close to me, her hand still gentle upon my shoulder, her eyes luminous and her lips inviting. It seems she is about to kiss me, but thinks better of it, hesitating and going still, neither of us daring to stir. Her scent, which I did not notice before, is intoxicating, stirring new thoughts within me. Our false embrace, which haunts the edges of my thoughts, ready to be called forth at an instant, returns, and this time the scent is added to the memory, and with it a feeling of longing.

My desire startles me. I have grown so used to thinking of Meredith as an adversary of some form that it is hard to think of her in any other way. I always found her beautiful, but now, for the first time, I am compelled to think upon that attraction, and perhaps to act. My feelings are at war with one another, my scant memories offering only confusion, and I find myself rising to my feet and moving away from her touch, frightened by the intensity of it all.

"I need some rest," I say, gesturing in the direction of the bedroom, the emotion making my voice raw.

Meredith nods, her face a mask again, though her eyes betray her sadness and disappointment. "Yes. That's good. Rest is good. We'll talk again at supper."

There is hurt in her voice, deep and inexpressible. It feels, as I walk away, my mind still in turmoil, like we have long been together, long shared these moments freighted with emotion and desire. The memory of our embrace, so charged with my anger and hurt at her betrayal, says as much. Yet what did she say that first day? *We were acquaintances.*

So much of what she said that day was half-truths and outright lies, intended, it seems to me now, to get me here where the Order has control of me, and where the Seeker, and all these others who are pursuing me, can't find me. Except that lie, the acquaintances, the casual friends, that seems as much to convince herself as anything, given the weight of history I now feel between us.

Now the question is, I think, as I throw myself upon my bed, closing my eyes to try to contain what lies within, is does she want that history, now submerged within me, to return, or to remain missing? And is that at war with whatever the Order and the Grand Regent want?

20

The woman slipped out of the building, drifting into the passing crowd on the street, and made her way west. I waited a moment, to ensure that she was going to keep heading that direction, before I detached myself from the entryway I had been seeking shelter under, and stepped out into the rain to follow her. The woman flipped a hood over her head, pulling the cloak she wore tight around her shoulders, making her difficult to pick out in a crowd full of people in similar dress, so I had to stay closer to her than I would have preferred.

At one point she stopped at a storefront, obviously checking to see if anyone was following her, and I wandered past, our shoulders almost brushing, and stepped into a shop selling religious icons. I made a show of studying their strange symbols, until I saw her pass by out of the corner of my eye. After forcing myself to count to five, I returned to the street and picked up the trail, spotting her at the next corner, just as she turned right. Halfway down the next block she darted through a break in traffic to the other side of the street. I stayed where I was, moving across the street and following her north at the next corner.

She led me on a roundabout path, doubling back on herself several times. She had to have noticed me with all her perambulations, yet she made no attempt to confront me or to deviate from her ultimate destination. It seemed strange to me that I was following her in secret, given that she had helped me only days before, though I understood this was but a memory or a dream. I had almost convinced myself she was no more than a phantasm, a result of whatever drugs De Vroes had given me, but evidently we had a past.

I was hard of purpose, aware of the danger of discovery. It was essential that I find out whom she was here to meet with. I knew who she was now, not some mere servant to the High Regent. The exact details of her position within the Church seemed to go vague the more I thought about them, but she was important, that much I understood. I had been ordered to follow her by the Grand Regent, and this was not the first time I had done so. There had been many times before.

The woman—her name still escaped me—led me to a tavern, its entryway descending from the street into a narrow, half-lit basement, lined with booths along one wall, a bar along the other, and a few scattered tables down the center. I did not follow her down the stairs, not wanting to risk being seen entering the establishment. Instead I went around back and, after some fumbling into the kitchen of a sushi place, found my way into the building and entered the tavern from the back, passing by the kitchen and into the main room with no one noticing. I went up to the bar and ordered a beer, nodding my head to the music playing, and scanned the room for the woman, spotting her in a booth deep in conversation with someone whose back was to me.

I sat in the booth next to them, casting my gaze on the front door, as though I was expecting someone, with my back to them. The walls on the booth were high so I would have no hope of watching them, but from my perch

I could just make out their conversation. As I had walked past I had been careful not to give so much as a glance in their direction, trying to glimpse the person with the woman from the corner of my eye. It was a man, I was quite certain, but I could not tell who, for his face was bathed in shadows.

The woman was speaking, her voice low, and I had to strain to hear it over the music. "This is the last time we can meet. I'm being watched."

"You were followed?" There was no reply, but I could almost see her nod and gesture at the booth I was sitting in and I froze in terror, expecting them both to confront me. Neither of them stirred from where they sat and the man said, "Are the flowers in bloom?"

"Given time, yes, the highlands will bloom," the woman replied.

"Good. When will it be time to harvest?" The man sounded excited, his voice rising. Again I felt the woman's gesture as she motioned for him to quiet his voice, could envision it completely. I could almost imagine her expression. It was as though I had two viewpoints upon the scene, one from where I sat listening to them, and one viewed from the corner of the booth where I could look upon them both.

"The harvest will come with the new moon. In the meantime, we shall have to keep an eye out for worms in the fruit."

"You think the harvest will spoil?"

"If we do not find the worms. It just takes one to spoil the whole, remember."

My breath felt as though it were about to burst from my chest, and I saw that my hands had clenched the table. The room seemed to swirl away for a moment, disappearing into a blur of darkness. It took me a moment to regain my equilibrium, and I wondered what was happening. It seemed something apart from the memory or dream I was experiencing, and I tried to fight my way to the surface of my consciousness to see what was happening, but found myself unable. The dream persisted and I could not awaken.

"I will take care," the man said. "What do you want me to do?"

"Do nothing," she said. "Be the loyal hand and work the field as always. I will send word when I can."

"I will be the faithful servant, then," the man said, and I felt a shiver of doom. "What shall the signal be?"

The woman spoke, but I did not hear what she said, for as she did, the lights returned in a ragged line, green and blue, flowering and overwhelming my sight. I clutched my head in agony, covering my eyes, until they subsided. When I opened them, the woman was staring at me, sitting across from me in the booth, recognition in her eyes and a sad and knowing smile on her face. It is that look that I do not forget even as I burst awake.

21

I am gasping for air as I crawl away, trying to escape from what I do not know, nearly falling off the bed in the process. The woman's face, her sad eyes, still loom in my mind. I can't bear the look of acceptance at my betrayal without accusation or malice. She helped me escape the High Regent and I betrayed her. I am caught in a maelstrom of emotion, revulsion and disgust at this body, this being, so powerful that I worry I will start retching upon the bed. I stumble to the bathroom and manage to splash some water on my face, which provides some relief, until I see the face looking back at me in the mirror.

The wrongness of the face strikes me like a blow. *Not this again*, I think, and duck from the bathroom, throwing myself back on the bed, squeezing my eyes shut and trying to calm my breathing.

I am David Aeida, I chant. *I am David Aeida*. The words feel empty and weak, their spell broken.

When I manage to regain my composure, I begin to assess where I am and what has happened to me. I am in the bedroom in the Watchers' Compound, though I can't recall when I went to bed or what time it is now. Outside the window is a vast darkness, a sky without stars. I fumble around for a clock, something to give me my bearings. Finding nothing, I go to my jacket and pull out my cell phone, only to discover the battery is dead.

Do they have a charger for it here? In all likelihood they will, but I do not want to give Meredith my phone. There might be something on it I don't want her to see.

I return the phone to my jacket and lie on the bed again, trying to fall asleep. Although I am exhausted, my eyes aching with fatigue, I cannot. I am afraid to dream again, afraid to lose what little of myself I have left. What will I remember when I wake up next? And what will I forget?

The distraction of my thoughts proves too great, and eventually I give up trying to sleep and got out of bed. I decide to go to the kitchen for some milk and go to my jacket to get my phone, thinking I will look for a charger while I am up and alone. As I slip my hand into the jacket, I encounter the weight of another object in an adjacent pocket. It has the shape of a flashlight, though when I pull it out to look at it closer, I can see it is not. I quickly search the other pockets and discover a tiny box with electrical cords of some sort extending from it. Struggle as I might, I cannot recall how or when I came into possession of these objects or what they are.

As I peer at them, turning them both over in my hands, I am suddenly conscious that I am almost certainly being watched, my every movement recorded and dissected by the Order. I return both objects to my jacket, deciding to wait until I can be sure I am not being observed before investigating them further. Will I be able to remember they are there? I can only hope.

On arriving in the kitchen, I realize the last thing I want is milk, and on a whim I descend below to the second level of the compound. If someone catches me, I reason, I can blame my insomnia and restlessness. It will also let me know how closely they are monitoring my movements.

I half expect an alarm to sound as I pass down the

stairs to the innocuous hallway that leads to what, at one time, was a recreation room, as well as some bedrooms. None do, and I hear nothing as I come to the landing and stand, poised to flee, listening for any signs of activity. The corridor is dark, though further on I can make out glimmers of light stealing out from beneath shut doors.

Drawn to them, I move down the hallway, not bothering to disguise my progress. If someone chances upon me I have no defense but my own delirium, which feels more real by the moment. Every time I halt my forward momentum and let my thoughts take hold of me, it feels as though I am losing what little grip upon myself I have. They are poisoning me, turning me into someone unsure of my own existence and that of the world around me.

As I approach the light at the end of the corridor I hear voices and creep forward, stopping before I come abreast of the doorway so that my shadow is not cast under it.

"...how would you describe her current status, then?" I catch only the last part of her question. It is a woman's voice, which I do not recognize, authoritative and blunt.

Meredith replies and I feel my whole body go tense. "I've seen no sign of her, as I said. My assumption is that things remain status quo for now."

"A dangerous assumption, as you well know."

There is a pause, and I can sense Meredith is considering her words carefully. "I do. I can assure you there's been no sign. I have not been the only sentinel on watch, as you know."

This appears to mollify the other woman. There is a long pause before she says, "Very well. I entrust it to your hands. See that you don't fail. And what of our patient?"

"I am concerned about him. He is displaying side effects."

Another lengthy pause follows, and I realize that it is not the woman considering her words but a delay in the feed, as though they are communicating across a vast distance. "What side effects, exactly? Do we know what Osahi did to him?"

"He will not tell me," Meredith says. "But I think they tried to remove the tamp. It doesn't look like they were successful, but he's become very disoriented. It's like he's...unsure of himself, I would say."

A wave of dizziness assaults me at the mention of my condition, and I have to reach out to touch the wall to stop myself from falling. For a terrifying moment I fear I will start retching in the hallway.

"You're certain his memories are repressed? It is essential that the tamp remain in place."

"I activated the..." I hear Meredith say before I have to walk away from the doorway.

The blood has gone from my head and my hands are suddenly so cold. I am worried that I will collapse where I stand. As I walk back down the corridor my pulse seems to return, along with my equilibrium, and I tell myself that I have to return and hear what they are saying. I have to know.

"Continue administering the suppressant when necessary," the other woman says.

I am being drugged. It would explain my endless sleep and exhaustion, as well as the gaps in my memory, and the collapsing synapses of my thoughts.

"Of course," Meredith says "What if the symptoms persist?"

"We will have to re-administer the tamp. It is essential that it remain in place. You know what the Grand Regent's feelings are in this matter."

"Yes, Acolyte," Meredith says. It feels as though their conversation is coming to a close. I turn and retreat back down the hallway, not daring to give in to temptation and try any of the doors, for fear of alerting Meredith to the fact I was listening to her.

As I return to my bedroom, passing upstairs through the living room and kitchen and down the hall, I notice a linen closet that somehow escaped my attention earlier. A low hum is being emitted from it and I open the door to investigate. Within, I can just make out through the shadows stacks of equipment, like computer mainframes bolted into the wall. Heat radiates off them and the air is heavy with undisturbed dust.

As it tickles my nose, drawing out a sneeze, a thought occurs to me. I go to my bedroom, retrieving my coat, and extract the two foreign objects from it. I shove them behind one of the mainframes, lower down on the stack where the dust is thick, ensuring they are safely out of view, before returning to my bedroom.

Sleep does not come, nor do I want it to, for I fear I will continue to forget, to return to that tabula rasa that Meredith and the Acolyte seem to desire me in. I can play that part, though, I tell myself, and if I play it well enough they might reduce whatever drugs they are giving me. Perhaps their surveillance as well. Then I will be free to make my escape.

22

"You seem lost," the man on the plaza said. "I can show you the way."

I glanced in his direction, a derisive phrase on my lips, which died when I met his eyes. He was wearing an expensive suit and shoes, and had a haircut, close-shaven and precisely etched, that looked as though it cost more than all the clothes I was wearing. Although, it was not as though that would be difficult to achieve in my current state. His appearance was completely at odds with his words, unless Vancouver yuppies had recently become proselytizers for some newly formed religion that I was unaware of, but his eyes were compelling and he held himself with such authority that my curiosity was piqued.

"Let me guess, you've found the secret to all existence," I said to him, "the answer to all my dreams and the way to make a million dollars and you'll sell it all to me for a price. Well, I'm not interested in money, friend."

"Clearly not," he said, sniffing with disdain as though the stench of my poverty was overpowering.

I was tempted to walk away, but something about his manner compelled me to stay. I had suffered enough humiliation these last three years, as I drifted across the country, from job to job, commune to collective, so what was a little more now?

"You're looking for something," he said, when it was clear that I was not leaving. "I can tell. I'm looking for something too. I'm going to bet it's the same thing."

"I doubt it," I said. "I'm just looking for something to eat."

"Why don't we see to that need first," he said, standing up. "And then we can go from there."

He took me to a sushi restaurant, where I gorged myself on nigiri and rolls while he picked sparingly at his udon bowl and talked non-stop about himself and his beliefs. His name, he told me, was Lasinha, and he spoke, I noticed now, with the hint of an accent I could not quite place. When I asked him where he was from he answered vaguely, which only furthered my suspicion that this was some sort of scam that I would have to extricate myself from before it went too far. Not until I had eaten my fill, though.

As he talked of multiple universes, infinite in variety, and one true universe of which we were all inadequate reflections, something stirred inside me. I had to admit I was intrigued by what he said. I could recall, from my aborted and flailing attempt at university, a physics professor talking about quantum mechanics and multiple universes, but it had been utterly beyond my comprehension. Now, though—and perhaps it was just Lasinha's innate charisma that made it so—it seemed to me there was a glimmer of truth in what he was saying. There was a reality beyond this one. We were but echoes in time. All the yearning, all the inchoate suffering I endured, finding satisfaction in none of what I did, it was all the result of being a regent to a true soul.

In my memory this soaring realization occurred during this first lunch with Lasinha, a surging crescendo of belief in the truth of his words seizing me as I first heard it. The reality was that my belief was formed over many distrustful weeks, Lasinha pursuing me, while I played hard to get, flirtatious one moment and distant the next. In the end he won out, his dogged effort bringing me into the fold. There was no singular moment, no word of God or parting of seas, when belief seized me, when I committed myself absolutely to the cause. For the first year I told myself I could abandon my new companions, this new faith, for something better at any time. For now it suited my needs, just as that first lunch had salved that hunger, only to reveal another deeper one I had been unaware of.

I let myself believe that the touch of faith had occurred during that lunch. In a way it was true, though the faith had not been mine. It was Lasinha, who in that hour had seen in me a worthy acolyte to be welcomed into the arms of the believers.

"The world is not what it seems, David," he said to me that day and many others.

No it is not, I think. *No it is not.*

"You're quiet today, are you feeling all right?" I glance up at Meredith, who just emerged from the second level of the compound, where she spent most of the morning. It is the first time she has done that since our arrival here, and I wondered if this is a sign of her growing trust in me or a test. Perhaps both.

"Just restless," I say to her with a half-smile.

Left to my own devices, I resisted the urge to look at the devices from the Seeker's car and instead spent the morning mulling my surfacing memories. They all feel so dreamlike I find myself wondering whether they are just my imagination working feverishly, trying to fit pieces together from all the fragments of thought that remain to me. Again and again I have the sensation, just as when I looked in the mirror, that these are not my thoughts, but someone else's.

"Sorry I haven't been around," Meredith says, sitting beside me. "There were just some things I had to attend to."

"Nothing serious, I hope."

"Me too," she says. We both seem wary of each other, I think, watchful and unsure of what the other person is going to do.

"Is there anything I can do to help?" I say. "I feel so useless just sitting here every day with nothing to do."

Meredith frowns. "I don't know. Without your memories...and I don't want to do anything that would bring them back."

Everything she says seems an evasion. "Would that really be so bad? Now that I'm safe here," I say, trying to keep the need from my voice.

They have to be memories, I tell myself; they feel real enough, and they have to be mine, no matter how foreign they seem. Memories are slippery things, after all, no more trustworthy than dreams. With the suppressants none of my thoughts can be trusted, sleeping or waking. For all I know these memories are side effects, or implants caused by the drugs.

Meredith reaches out to take my hand. *She is trying to establish trust,* a voice in my mind says. It is a comfort, I cannot deny.

"I can't imagine how it must feel to have no memory. To not be sure of who you are," she says. "But we have to be very careful right now. Until we can be sure that we can get you over, we don't want your memory coming back."

"It's about the impossible universe isn't it. That's what I know and that's why everyone wants it."

Meredith shrugs her shoulders, making every effort to be as casual as possible. "I can't say. I'm sorry. It doesn't matter anyway. Right now I'm only worried about keeping you stable."

"If I had something to do it would keep my mind off it," I say. "It doesn't have to be anything important. I could clean up here. Prepare meals, whatever. I must have done something for the past eight months."

"We found you a job," Meredith says, leaning back and pursing her lips. "Yes. Why don't you do some chores around here. I can put together a list of things to be done, if you'd like. There are even some places downstairs you could clean. Maybe some other stuff."

She seems excited as she thinks more about it. "This is good," she says, looking at me with a smile. "This is good." I smile in return.

Good, you have her trust, now see what you can gain by it. My hand begins to shake and I hide it at my side.

It feels like days since I slept. Perhaps it was; I can no longer recall. The days all look the same, mist-filled and dreary, the clouds breaking only for an hour or two each afternoon. I have lost track of how long I have been in the Watchers' compound, the empty routine of my days wearing at the edges of my recall as surely as the torture of my sleepless nights.

I dream—even though I cannot sleep, I dream. Or have visions. Voices speak to me, whisper insidiously between my thoughts. I am slowly coming apart at the seams, I realize, and there seems nothing I can do about it. Meredith appears not to notice, and I do all I can to hide my anguish from her.

Wait for your chance, the voice whispers. I have grown to suspect it, for it is not my interior voice. It is distinct, another entity entirely. Is it leading me astray?

I try to ignore it for the most part, to ignore the dreams, the memories, all so confusing and fragmented, and to live in the now. I clean the house daily, compulsively dusting and scrubbing sparkling floors and countertops as though they are marred with stains that cannot be removed. Meredith watches me, offering no comment on my effort, though I can feel her nervousness growing as she wonders if my obsessions will somehow give bloom to some strange fruit.

Sometimes I wonder about what it is I know that could

be so important they would do this to me and I would agree to it. It has to be important, significant. It has to be worth all this agony and misery. Most of the time I hate the fact that fate has chosen me to possess it and long for it to be destroyed, even if I am obliterated in the act.

When I am done with my chores, usually sometime in the early afternoon, I head to the living room to stare out the windows down the mountainside. Most days there is little to see, the clouds and mist surround the compound, cutting it off entirely from the rest of the world. I imagine that Meredith brought me to some lost kingdom that exists in another universe from the one I live in. Perhaps it is true, for how else have they hidden me from the Seeker all this time?

Time certainly seems to pass differently here, though that has more to do with my own altered state of mind. These long waking endless hours, one after the other, my thoughts at war with themselves.

23

Something has happened, I can tell by the expression on Meredith's face and the careful, guarded way in which she speaks to me.

"Get your things together," she says. "We may have to leave very quickly."

I have no things, I want to tell her, except the clothes that she's given me, but I just nod and said I will. As I go to find a bag to pack some clothes in, I wonder if this is a trick to force me to reveal the hiding place for the objects I hid. That seems unlikely. If they are aware of them, a search will just as easily lead to their discovery. Which means I should take them with me, for who knows if I will ever return to this compound. I desperately hope not.

Lasinha became my guiding star; for over a year I set my path by his word. We would meet often, at first just to talk as he explained the principles of the faith and our work in this universe. He would ask me questions as well, about my life and what had brought me to him. Often he would ask me the same questions over and over again, day after day, noting down what I said. This was part of a process called the pre-script. The script of my life before I came to understand the true nature of the universes. This would lead to something called the Protocols, which would be my induction to the faith.

Lasinha promised that it would not be long before I would take the Protocols, but first my mind had to be made ready. Meanwhile, he introduced me to the other faithful in the universe. Services were held off and on at a small multi-faith church in a neighborhood east of Chinatown. Lasinha was the only one from the other world and he led the services, teaching us the prayers and songs, the rituals of the faith.

When people asked about the services we told them we were Scientologists or Raelians. We were not to proselytize; Lasinha was very clear on the matter. There were others from the other universe who did not look kindly on our faith, and they were watching the other worlds for signs of the Church. We had to be careful.

Meredith is standing at the door to my bedroom, an odd expression on her face. I look at her, confused. How long has she been there? I was mulling whether to bring the objects when I became lost in my thoughts. Was I speaking aloud? It feels as though an abrupt silence has fallen, interrupting some conversation. There is no one here but myself, though, and whatever memory I stumbled into in my waking reverie.

"We have to go now," Meredith says, piercing the clatter of my thoughts.

"I'm almost ready," I say, thinking of the objects still hidden in the closet.

"No, there's no time."

Meredith leads me below to the third level of the compound. I look open-eyed at everything, for I have never ventured here, even in my most daring of nighttime explorations. The entirety of the third floor is within the mountain and was clearly developed by the Order. Its look, its feel, even its smell is distinct from all that lies above, and none of the luxury and comfort that marks the other rooms exists here. The walls and floor are bare concrete, and I imagine our footsteps echoing down the hallway.

We come to one doorway and then another, each sealed and guarded by a keypad. Meredith has the code and we pass through, the door sealing behind us, and we go further into the mountain as images of tombs enter my mind. My breath begins to feel short and my knees weak. Meredith grabs me by the arm to steady me, not saying a word.

On we go into a labyrinth of intersecting tunnels, all of which look the same, low lit and narrow. There is no apparent purpose to them that I can discern, other than to disorient me, for there appears to be no rooms leading off the hallways, no doorways that lead elsewhere, and seemingly no end to the tunnels. How deep into the mountain do they go? We must, I think, be almost across the street by now. Meredith chooses her path without thought, as though she has traversed these byways many times before.

Our path becomes so tangled that I begin to wonder if we are lost and if Meredith's apparent confidence is nothing more than a bluff intended to set me at ease.

"Where are we going?" I say, my voice sounding hollow to my ears.

Just as I speak the words, a light appears ahead of us, coming from the ceiling down into the end of the corridor we are upon. Meredith freezes in her tracks, throwing up a hand to stop me from going any further. The light is in a thin, focused beam, though it is expanding by the moment, and white in color. As the beam widens it becomes painful to look at, and the faint odor of smoke reaches us. I take an unsteady step forward, fascinated by the light and what it is doing, which brings Meredith back to herself.

She grabs me by the arm and pulls me back, starting to

run in the other direction. "We have to go," she says. "We have to go."

There are shouts behind us as we start to run, spurring us both on as we flee back the way we came.

Each of us, the followers of Lasinha—though we called ourselves Regents, it was he whom we worshiped—had duties and tasks to complete. I never knew what the others did and kept my own work secret. Lasinha preferred it that way, and when Ana came she continued with the practice. For all of us, it was a way to create the illusion we were his favorite, bound to him with secrets only we shared.

Perhaps everyone else felt the same, but I believed Lasinha entrusted me with more faith than any of the others. Certainly we spent more time together. He would get his messages from the other world and find me and together we would gather what we needed and send it "across the great divide," as Lasinha referred to it.

"Come on," Meredith says. "We have to go."

She sounds desperate, her voice strained with emotion, and it looks as though she is choking back tears. I look around, trying to regain my bearings, and see that we are still in the tunnels beneath the compound. In the distance I can just make out the sinister gleam from the light that penetrated the corridors from above.

"Come on," Meredith says to me again. "They'll be through any minute."

I hesitate, unsure of what I should do, my thoughts seeming to vanish and reappear at odd angles. *You cannot stay here,* the voice says, but I do not trust it. A terrifying sound, high-pitched and grinding, like a saw cutting at itself, reverberates toward where we stand, deciding my course of action. Relief washes over Meredith's face and we begin to run.

24

The quiet seems ominous. I am afraid to move, lest I shatter the absolute stillness that has descended upon the compound. There is no hum of electricity, no dull hush of air being circulated through vents, no sigh of mysterious equipment starting or stopping that marked all my days here. The hidden sounds that make up the background of a life in the world. They have all disappeared and now we find ourselves faced with our own disappearance.

I look across at Meredith and she will not meet my eyes. We are barricaded in a room on the third floor just past the tunnels that whoever penetrated the compound is now making their way through. How long will it take them to navigate that labyrinth? Not long, judging by the panic Meredith is trying hard to disguise. And with the power cut it will not be difficult to break into our sanctuary. *You cannot stay here*, the voice says to me. I swallow, trying to ignore its whispers, trying to think of something to say, afraid to break the silence.

Cell phone parts, computer circuit boards, and other electronic equipment that we had salvaged or stolen were sent over in packages, as well as copper wiring, coffee beans, and other oddities. What all these things had to do with each other and the search for the one true universe I could not fathom, nor did I ask Lasinha, and he volunteered no explanation.

Meredith appears to have entered a state of shock. She looks blankly at me as a rumble of sound reaches us from within the mountain. What it signifies I can only guess. *You cannot stay here*, the voice repeats. I am David Aeida, I tell myself, and that voice is not me. It does not matter, though; I know it is correct. We are doomed if we stay, we have to act, but Meredith is incapable of anything at the moment.

I take her by the hand. "We have to go."

"There's nowhere to go," she says. "They have the place surrounded. They've cut off the escape tunnels."

"Who?"

She shrugs as though it does not matter. Thoughts stutter through my head and I blink, trying to find some focus. I think I can hear voices echoing down the corridor toward us, but I hope I am just imagining things.

Meredith glances up at the sound as well, and I know, with a sinking feeling, that it has not just been in my head. A terrible clarity seizes her and she takes my hand in hers, clutching it and staring at me with mournful eyes.

"I have failed you," she says. "I am so sorry. Can you forgive me?"

The weight with which she says these words gives me pause. I stare at her blankly, wondering what she is talking about, for it seems to me she is referring to much more than just our present situation. This is a settling of debts that I have no way of reckoning.

It cannot be the Society, the voice says to me, *the Seeker cannot find the compound, unless you turn the cloaking off.*

"Isn't the cloaking device already off with the power gone?" I say aloud, drawing a look of concern from Meredith. It is not enough to rouse her from her stasis.

Turn the cloaking off, the voice says, *flood the chambers and let the Seeker come.* Are these things that I somehow know, that my memory is restoring to me, or are they someone else's thoughts? It's impossible for me to judge. All I know is that it is unlikely to be side effects from the suppressants. Side effects do not have plans.

The metals made sense to me; perhaps they were needed for the crossing-over mechanisms or some of the other foreign technology I had glimpsed Lasinha using. The Church lived a rationed existence on the other side, as I understood it, though Lasinha seemed to have unlimited wealth in this world, so all these odds and ends might be intended to help that. I did not ask. I was simply glad to be involved.

There is a loud, indeterminate clatter of metal upon concrete, dim and distant, but seemingly nearer and more tangible than the sounds we heard before. The sound decides it for me, and I get to my feet, holding out my hand to Meredith.

"We have to go," I say. When she doesn't respond, I reach down and roughly pull her to her feet. She looks as though she wants to hit me but manages just to swallow her emotions.

"We're going," I say to her firmly. "You have to show me where the cloaking room is."

She nods and, without looking at me, leads the way from the room.

Each step seems to require an act of will, a battle to remember where I am, what I am doing, and to fight off the memories that are erupting within me. I fear being swallowed in remembering, the pleasure and regret of times past, to lose myself to it completely. The voice, relentless as always, will not allow me. It pierces my thoughts, shattering the seductive reverie...

The mechanism of crossing over continually fascinated me. Lasinha tried to keep the particulars obscure, but he could not resist telling me some of what he knew. To hide what we were doing from the Society of Travelers, we would include some objects that were from the other universe in each transfer—for example, the crate on which the objects were sent—while simultaneously people on the other side would send objects of the same weight across to us, including substances from both worlds.

One step in front of the other, like a wandering drunkard I go forward, clutching at Meredith when my balance is threatened. She says something to me, her voice frantic and hoarse…

It was trickier with people, Lasinha noted; unless you somehow managed to switch the same individual there would be two of them wandering about the same world. But the principle was the same, an exchange of weight, most often an exchange of people, one person coming and the other going. Any close inspection by a Society member or a Seeker would reveal that the person was not of the world they were in, but first they had to notice that the transfer had taken place. The Church, Lasinha told me, had people in the Society, knew their transfer schedule, and could time their harmonics to match those of the Travelers, so that any transfer they made would be disguised as residual energy.

In theory, but a thousand things could go wrong, as Lasinha never failed to say, and the hours following the exchanges were always nerve-racking as we awaited the all-clear from the other side.

The noises below us cease, which I know is ominous. Whoever it is has entered the compound and will now be making their way toward us. I have no idea where we are—the third floor or the second—or where we are going. Meredith is saying something, but I can't hear her. I stare at her dumbly, unsure of what we are doing. The voice is trying to speak but I can't hear it over the din in my head. Meredith screams and I blinked at her in surprise.

The world is not real, it is folded in on itself, doubled and tripled. The fabric of existence has been torn into shards that I can't begin to stitch together. My thoughts are not my own; this is the only thing I can be certain of. All that I perceive is potentially a lie, just like the sweet whispers I shared with Meredith, her honeyed lips brushed with poison, slow-working but inexorable. Will she give me the antidote in time?

I have been in this place before. There are rooms here where unspeakable things were done. Why can I not remember them? Because that is the unspeakable thing. The thought hits me with a brutal clarity. It has all been taken from me.

I turn and start to run, Meredith calling out to me, "No. David, come back."

The universe spins on its axis at her words. I am David Aeida. The voice is insistent, but I cannot understand it, the words garbled and misshapen, a strange and foreign tongue...

One day I went to meet Lasinha at our usual place, a bar along West Broadway, and he was not there. I waited for an hour, nursing a beer, for I still did not have much in the way of money, before giving up and leaving. The next week Ana was there to meet me, beautiful and mysterious. Lasinha had been called over to the other universe and I was now to work with her. If it had been anyone else but her I would have abandoned the cause, unwilling to commit to this strange religion without my mentor to guide me. Ultimately I believed in Lasinha, not the Church, but Ana was so intoxicating I stayed just for the chance that maybe something would happen.

Meredith is pulling my arm as I strain against her in a frenzy to escape. She is not to be trusted. My body ached everywhere like I took a tumble down some stairs. My ears are ringing. Did an explosion go off? What is happening?

Find the cloaking device, the voice says. *Turn it off.*

These are not my thoughts, they are someone else's. I redouble my efforts to escape Meredith. She proves much stronger than I, refusing to let go of my arm, pulling me in closer so that she falls on me, putting her slight weight firmly upon my body. The curve of her hips, the scent of her hair and her breath, warm on my cheek, stuns me momentarily, drawing me away from myself. My flesh responds to her touch in a way my thoughts seem incapable of forming. How many times did we lie so against each other? It is all so familiar.

"Please," Meredith says, her voice trembling in desperation. "We have to go. They're going to kill us."

As she speaks I can hear shouts from the floor below. Command and response. An invasion force. The orders and Meredith's fear sparks something in me and I react, my body acting under some strange compulsion not my own. I push her aside and rise to my feet, looking about to get my bearings. We are on the second floor of the compound, near the stairs that lead both above and below, which is why we can hear the sounds of ours pursuers so clearly. Who are they? Osahi's recruits or some other players unknown as yet to me?

It doesn't matter. I turn to Meredith, who has risen to her feet and is standing, watching me with unsteady eyes. "Where is the cloaking device?"

She looks at me, her eyes edged with fear, which I can well understand. The voice in which I spoke is not my own.

25

Meredith leads me to the main floor of the compound and the closet beside my bedroom where earlier I hid the Seeker's implements. She gestures to it, saying nothing, edging away from me as I throw open the door. I can well understand her wariness; I am frightened of myself at this moment.

My thoughts are shifting second by second. One instant I am trapped in the past, reliving the vagaries of David Aeida's existence, the next I am being attacked from all sides, unsure of who I even am, all while the voice continues its insidious whispers. It is another entity within me, cajoling and entreating me, seductive in its absolute certainty.

I turn to her as I study the shelves of what, at first glance, appears to be servers, though I now recognize what they are. "Go hit the kill switch," I say in my voice, now cold and authoritative.

Meredith hesitates, unsure of herself. She appears helpless to do anything in the face of this latest assault, the hard veneer of competence she maintained crumbling in its face. Why that should be the case now when she faced down the Seeker without so much as blinking, I cannot imagine.

"There is a kill switch in every compound. I know there is," the voice says through me. I am watching myself from a portal in the corner of my eye, as disbelieving as Meredith is. "You said they were going to kill us. Then we don't have a choice, do we?"

"No," Meredith said at last, and reluctantly turned to go back down the hallway.

I watch her go, waiting until she disappears around the corner before I reach into the closet, digging behind the cloaking devices to pull out the Seeker's implements, stuffing them into my jacket pockets. Next I turn my attention to the cloaking device, whose fans continue to whir in spite of the power being cut. I look blankly at the stacks of equipment, unsure where to begin. The whispers direct me to what appears to be a circuit box attached to one of the side walls. A series of cables, strung along the wall from the cloaking devices, penetrates the box, which, when I pry it open, reveals a warren of wires and circuit boards.

Pull the circuits, the voice says, and I do, yanking them free of the box and its wires. There is no immediate change that I can discern; the fans continue to whir in the devices and the lights on the various boxes all continue to glow. Gradually I begin to feel a shift in the air, a tingle upon the edges of my skin, the atmosphere charged as though in a storm. Setting the circuits on the floor, I smash them under the heel of my shoe. *Burn all the boats.*

I find Meredith in the kitchen, her hand hovering over what looks to be the thermostat, poised to strike, her face clouded in doubt. The command and response reemerges from below. They have finished their sweep of the first floor and moved on to the second. We don't have much time.

"You have to press it," I say to Meredith, this in my own quavering voice.

She turns to face me, her hand dropping away, emotion

overwhelming her expressions. "There are Regents down there. Our people."

I shrug, trying to ignore the ever-growing sounds of the intruders. "We left Osahi to his fate."

"That was different. There are Watchers down there. The compound hasn't been evacuated."

I feel the blood drain from my face at the thought of untold numbers perishing just to spare us. It is the voice that speaks next. "There's no one down there. There hasn't been anyone down there since we arrived. The only people we'll be killing are the extraction squad."

Meredith bites her lip. "There has to be another way," she says, her old fierceness returning. "We can escape somehow."

"You know there isn't. They have the compound surrounded, and now that the cloaking device is off we're about to have a lot of company. They can't find me here. You know that. Osahi was near enough to a disaster. If they take me over..."

I allow my words to trail off and Meredith slouches, all the energy draining from her as quickly as it returned. "I won't be responsible for the murder of other Regents," she says.

"It's a little late for that now," the voice says, and she looks at me, the fear returning to her eyes.

She steps away from the thermostat, her surrender complete. I thrust my way past her, the voice muttering through my thoughts about her cowardice, and look at the keypad hidden beneath the thermostat casing. She entered the code already; all that remains is to execute the command. I stretch out my hand and press the button, triggering an immediate reaction throughout the compound. An alarm begins to sound below, and a moment later the stairway is sealed over by a thick metal panel, some foreign alloy I do not recognize. When it locks in place, sealing the extraction squad below, the alarm goes silent. Meredith and I stand, each of us unwilling to move, mute with dread, waiting for what is to come next.

The quiet extends on for what seems like minutes, until at last I hear something that sounds distant, from far below and deep within the mountain. I don't recognize it at first and find myself straining to make out what it is, until a sick realization comes over me. They are screaming. It seems endless but lasts no more than a terrible few minutes. Meredith and I do not look at each other the entire time it lasts, neither of us acknowledging what we are hearing.

When it is at last over and the tension and anguish has leaked away from both of us, leaving only an awful emptiness, I descend from the kitchen to the living room to look out the windows at the mountain and all that lies below. For the first time since my arrival, the rain has stopped and the cloud and mist have started to dissipate. I can just make out the blue gleam of the ocean as the sun strikes it. *It will not be long now.*

Just as the voice speaks there is a thud at the door, followed by a crash as it bursts open. A half-dozen men enter, their weapons at the ready.

FOUR:

A FINE VESSEL

26

The remainder of the extraction squad glowers at Meredith and I as they surround us, their weapons leveled at our chests. They are wearing armored vests and helmets with tactical visors that cover the entire upper halves of their faces, adding to their ominous effect. The weapons I do not recognize—pulse guns of some sort, the voice suggests. They are a glittering obsidian and hum slightly as the men rest their fingers on the triggers. I resist the urge to let my hands stray to my own coat, where the Seeker's implements are. That is a sure recipe to be shot.

Not long now.

I feel lightheaded and blink, turning again to look down the mountain at the glistening sea. Downtown is now visible, the high rises looking like molten silver towers wavering in the atmosphere.

"Don't move," one of the extraction squad shouts at me. He sounds very young, his voice strained and nervous. I turn to look at him, raising an eyebrow, and he levels his weapon at my eyes. The commander waves a gentle hand at him, urging calm, and gestures for two others to conduct a survey of the other rooms.

"Identify yourselves," he says, sweeping the room as he

does so. The two remaining soldiers stay where they are, their weapons trained on Meredith and I.

"We have nothing to say to you," Meredith says, her voice marked with scorn. "This is an illegal incursion. You have violated the Regency Charters."

"Shut up," the commander says. "You're in no position to lecture others on unlawful activities." He stops by the stairway, tapping his foot on the panel that seals it off. "What did you do?" he says.

"What we had to do," Meredith says. In spite of the bravado in her voice, her face tells a different story, doubt and anguish plainly visible, at least to my eyes.

"You'll answer for this. I'll see to it."

Meredith doesn't answer him, and I return my gaze to the mountains and the city below, now fully visible, the cloud evaporated, the day glorious. I try not to think about the screams, feeling unsteady on my feet. A scatter of memories bursts forth from my subconscious, only to vanish before I can parse them, leaving only an aching absence. The wound of my thoughts.

"They were of the faith. Regents," the commander is shouting at Meredith.

She doesn't look at him. "You were going to kill us. It was you or us."

"*We* don't kill fellow Regents," the commander snarls. "By De Gofroy, I'll see that you die for this."

Not long now, the voice repeats, sounding more plaintive, as if begging me to hold on a moment more. I blink rapidly, trying to focus on the city below, the mountain, even as it becomes a blur, a kaleidoscope of color. It is difficult to breathe.

"Now, by the power vested in me by the Regency Charters, I command you to identify yourselves," the commander shouts.

Meredith allows a small smile to pass across her lips. "You're already doomed, you just don't know it."

The commander seems about to say more, but the two

men he sent to search the rest of the floor return.

"The place is empty," one of them says.

"We found this in the hallway," the other says, passing the commander the remnants of the circuit board I pulled from the cloaking device.

The commander holds it up to his visor, trying to determine what it is and where it came from. Realization slowly dawns on him and he drops the circuit. "We have to move," he says to the others.

"You're too late," Meredith says.

"Another word from you," the commander says, pointing a finger at her, "and I swear I will kill you here and now."

He waves for the others to follow him and heads toward the door. "Full alert," he calls out, pointing for the two men who just returned to fan out, which they do, weapons at the ready. The other two grab Meredith and I roughly by the shoulders, pressing their guns into our backs, pushing us toward the door.

I stumble forward, my legs seemingly incapable of functioning. There is a strange metallic taste in my mouth and the world spins and then stops.

27

For two lovelorn years I followed Ana, giving myself to her completely, though I knew heartbreak could be the only result. She seemed to exude an alluring darkness, her eyes dark hypnotizing pools and her hair long waves of a dark sea I wanted to wash over me. Did she enjoy leading me on? Was she even aware of my feelings? I both hated and longed for her, railed against the Church for taking Lasinha from me, and embraced it totally, trying to subsume my obsession for Ana with belief. I failed in that, my doubts still remaining and my feelings for Ana growing only powerful the more I tried to deny them.

She was careful to keep her distance from me, especially in the beginning. Unlike Lasinha, who had worked hard to create a bond between himself and all his recruits, one that tied us to him as much as to the Church, Ana assumed we were all tied together by our belief in the True Faith and made no apparent effort to engage us. She was our Adjudicator and we would obey her commands, because as followers of the faith it was expected of us.

I bridled at such expectations, just as I had my whole life. Lasinha had recognized it in me and had crafted his teachings of the True Faith in such a way as to appeal to this sensibility in me. In his casting of it, I was not some mere minor officiant who saw to obscure and unimportant rituals of the faith, but a part of a band of outsiders in a struggle against a nefarious authority in the shape of the Society of Travelers.

Ana made no such allowances for my vanity, which angered me to no end. I would rail against her whenever my duties or the ceremonies of the Church would draw me into the path of my fellow Regents. They would listen politely, with pained expressions, and murmur vague agreements, before moving to extract themselves from my presence. It was as though they understood, in a way I never could, that my anger had nothing to do with the way Ana governed the Church in our universe. My rage was some noxious elixir derived from my hurt at Lasinha abandoning me—he had not even let me know he was going, after all—and the transmutation of my longing for her.

In spite of my tortured feelings, the misery I allowed myself to fall into—which in truth only made my desire more intoxicating—I continued with all I had done for Lasinha. Ana soon trusted me enough that I was often left to handle the exchanges across the universes myself, so that I became quite expert. At some point, I realized that I knew as much as she did about the workings of the Society and our efforts to subvert its controls, if not more.

"You are indispensable David Aeida," she would say with a smile and the air would go from my lungs.

It was high praise coming from her, for she seemed to view the inhabitants of our universe, including those of us who had joined the faith, as little more than rubes, ignorant of the nature of the universes and the laws that governed them. How must she feel, I wondered, forced to live among so many who could not possibly understand the world as she knew it was? That, I told myself, was the reason she did not share my desire and longing. I was irreparably stained by being of this universe. No matter how often I might prove myself to be indispensable, I would always be of this place where she did not want to be.

She never gave voice to such thoughts—she was far too much the professional for that—but I was sure I could detect their undercurrents in all that she said. Duty was her watchword, she talked of it endlessly, rarely touching on the belief that was central to our faith. It seemed to make her uncomfortable.

I asked her once what had drawn her to the Church and she had been confused by my question. "I was born into it," she said. "My parents were some of De Gofroy's first converts. The universes cannot be other than they are for me. I have always known that the impossible one awaits us."

She seemed insulted by my question and I never dared to pry into her past again. I imagined it though, her life in De Gofroy's universe, growing up amongst the faithful. I could not help but be jealous of the surety of her belief and of her place with the chosen, for I had never felt it. Doubt had marked all my days and doubt in her, and in myself, would be my undoing.

28

I see Meredith first, hovering over me, a specter come to visit my nightmares. My throat is dry, my tongue heavy with the taste of metal. The others come into view after a moment: the extraction squad sprawled upon the compound floor—unconscious or dead, I cannot tell.

"Come on," Meredith says, "we've only got a minute before they're here."

I look at her, unable to comprehend what she is referring to. My thoughts seem hopelessly confused, part of me still lost in the memory that just overtook me. Is Ana the woman who helped me escape from the High Regent? No, she does not look like that woman and has none of her mannerisms. But I was so confused—and under the influence of drugs and whatever procedure De Vroes performed on me—that I can't say for certain they are not the same person. Ana feels familiar to me, now that the memory of her has returned, though I am not sure what that might mean.

Meredith interrupts my thoughts. "Come on. He'll be here any second. If we're going to go we have to go now."

I look at her, the clouds parting in my mind for the moment, and say, "That was never the plan."

She looks startled and takes a step back from me. As she does the front door bursts open and the Seeker enters followed by two Black Robes. The Seeker casts his eyes across the room, taking the entire scene in at a glance and nods to himself.

"Bring them," he says, pointing at us.

"What about these others?" one of the Black Robes says, gesturing at the extraction squad.

"Leave them," the Seeker says. "They're not going anywhere. We've closed off this world. We can deal with them later."

One of the Black Robes steps down into the living room and beckons for us to step toward them. He is new, I think, though they all seem to look of a piece: broad-shouldered, square-headed, and menacing. But one of them—Asdrubal, the name comes to me—was killed in their battle with the High Regent, replaced by this man, apparently. How many of them are there, I wondered—Seekers and Travelers, Regents and Watchers? There seems an endless supply of people who can cross over, and yet I somehow failed in my attempt and it has brought me nothing but ruin and death.

This all began well before that though, I now realize. The bits and pieces of memory that are slowly returning to me confirm that much. Lasinha and Ana, they are a part of it, my first steps on the path that led me here. I am beginning to understand my place in all this, though I can see nothing as yet that would point to any particular importance that I have in the Church or the Order. I don't understand how it fits within the Church and I within it. Most important of all, whatever knowledge I possess, that the Grand Regent wants protected, remains lost in the void, still to emerge.

I can only hope. I desperately need it to if I am going to survive. It is the only card I have to play. Meredith and those in the Order will not harm me so long as they know it remains within me, and it is the only leverage I have with the other factions in the Church, and perhaps with the Seeker himself.

The Black Robe beckons again. I see it dimly, as though from another place, and my thoughts swam with the murk of childhood and glimpses of long forgotten moments, of delight and strife, all unconnected. Meredith has already gone up the stairs and stands, cowering, by the Seeker, not daring to meet his alien eyes. The Black Robe gestures and says something, but I don't hear it. I see him turn back to look at the Seeker, who is watching with evident curiosity.

I am unable to move—it seems a miracle to me that I am even standing—my body numb, as if it is lost in sleep. Everything lies just beyond my comprehension. The Seeker's arrival, and all that followed, is jumbled in my thoughts, with all these memories that seem to consume me. It is as though I am living each of these moments again. They all feel new.

"Come," the Seeker commands, his voice seeming to fill the room, and my body at last responds, as it wouldn't to my own thoughts.

Do not look in his eyes. A command.

I follow Meredith up the stairs and out the door, the Seeker leading the way, one of the Black Robes falling in behind. We are taken to what appears to be the same car I stole earlier and ushered into the back, the Black Robe sitting between us, while the Seeker sits in the passenger seat. The remaining Black Robe shuts the door to the Watchers' compound and attaches something to it—from where we sit on the street I can't tell what, though intuitively I know it is intended to seal the door, trapping the extraction team within—before getting into the driver's seat. He starts the engine, which hums as quietly as before, and, with a glance at the Seeker who nods, we are underway.

29

It was toward the end of her second year in our universe that Ana began to take a greater interest in me. After so many weeks of leaving the exchanges with the other universes to me to handle she began to attend them, overseeing my work and taking careful notes on all that was transferred back and forth, as though she expected an audit to be forthcoming. Though I wondered what had sparked this sudden curiosity, I did not dare to ask Ana about it, for fear that it would end as quickly as it had begun.

After several weeks of this, each one of which I savored (and hated myself for doing so), Ana announced that we would be changing the location of the next exchange. When I asked her why she said, "We have been using this place since Lasinha's time."

"Yes," I said, though it had not been a question.

"It is poor protocol to continue to use the same location. It increases our chances of discovery."

Lasinha had never mentioned this to me, and it seemed like the kind of information that would be essential for someone coordinating the exchanges, but I did not argue with her. There had been many things Lasinha had kept from me, not least his leaving, and this was perhaps another.

"I will call you with the location once we have established it," Ana told me, which I also found perplexing. Should I not be involved in the selection of the site, given I had much more knowledge of this Vancouver than her?

It was all very out of the ordinary, but the next exchange passed without incident at the new location and I settled into the new routine at the new place, an abandoned office above a coffee shop. This came to an abrupt conclusion a little over a month later, when Ana told me that I was not needed at the next exchange.

"Have I done something wrong?" I said, trying and failing to keep the hurt from my voice.

"No," she said. "You have been indispensable. I just can't have you at the next exchange. After that things will return to normal. But we'll be moving to a new place."

I looked at her, but her face, as always, was remote and her expression unreadable. "Are we having problems with the Travelers?" I said.

"Perhaps. I'm not entirely sure what is going on."

"Then why all these changes in procedure?" I sounded aggrieved, but I could not help it. Lasinha had always kept me in the dark, and I had known he was doing it and accepted it as a matter of course. With Ana I could not. Each thing she kept from me was not a matter of protocol, but a rejection of me. I could not view our relationship through any other lens but that of my unrequited desire.

"Call it an abundance of caution, nothing more," she said with a kind smile, suggesting she understood my hurt feeling, which only made the cut run deeper.

"Don't you trust me?" I said.

"I have no doubts about you, David Aeida," Ana said. "In fact, the reason I want you away from here is for your own protection. Things are happening."

"What kind of things?"

She hesitated, seeming to debate whether or not to say more. "I can't really say for sure. Rumors mostly from the other side. I've heard there are people whose memories are being erased or suppressed. Regents. And that someone within the Church is doing it."

I stared at her, trying to understand what she was saying and what it implied. "Why would anyone do that?"

Ana shook her head. "I don't know. Best to take care with who you trust though, David Aeida. Your friends may not be your friends."

30

We wind our way down the mountain, finding our way onto a freeway, and eventually crossing a bridge back into the main part of the city. It is a glorious day, hardly a cloud in the sky, and people wander the streets in t-shirts and shorts. I am oblivious to the passing scenery and to where we are heading, though I can sense Meredith alert to all our twists and turns on the other side of the car. I have the feeling it will not matter in the end.

I entertain no fantasies of escape, keeping my eyes directly on the seat in front of me while I try not to think about the man sitting in it. He is thinking about me though, and eventually he shifts in his seat and turns around. I do not look up from my intensive study of the car's upholstery, but I can feel his gaze upon me as he cranes his neck. On the other side of the car Meredith goes very still, no doubt resisting the urge to look over and be drawn into the orbit of the Seeker's eyes.

My palms are damp with sweat, made worse by the pressing of the two objects concealed in my jacket against my arms. The Black Robes did not search me. Is it possible they are unaware anything was been taken from the car? Or do they simply not view them or me as a threat?

They are arrogant above all else. The voice offers little comfort, for it will take only a question from the Seeker for me to reveal my theft.

"We meet again, strange one," the Seeker says, finding some amusement in the fact. "It seems all the universes are looking for you."

"I'm beginning to wonder," I manage to say.

"We have nothing to say to you," Meredith says, "until we are in the presence of an advocate."

I can feel the Seeker's gaze leave me and turn upon Meredith, and I allow myself a quick glance up. His face is impassive as always, though his lips are curved into a mirthless smile.

"I can certainly send you across and arrange for counsel to be provided," he says to Meredith. "You can answer for your crimes there. But this one is of this world. By Society protocol, and the law of our Earth, we cannot violate the sanctity of the universes by transposing him. We would be guilty of the same crime he attempted to commit. But I can send you and he can remain with me."

Meredith does not reply, and the Seeker chuckles to himself. "I take it you choose to remain here."

He turns back to me, and I feel an overwhelming compulsion to submit to him and meet his gaze. *Do not look at him*, the voice commands. I turn away, looking outside at the passing street, trying to focus on the individuals I see there.

"You are learning," the Seeker says. "Or perhaps your memory has returned."

"It comes and goes," I say, shifting uncomfortably in the seat. I can feel Meredith staring at me as well, willing me to be silent.

"Difficult times for you," the Seeker says. "Not understanding who you are and your place in all this, not knowing who you can trust, and these cultists filling your mind with their nonsense and conspiracies."

I can feel the Seeker's attention shift to Meredith to see

if she will respond to his slights. She keeps her peace, though I can feel her ire growing.

"You are very perceptive, Mr. Aeida," the Seeker says. "Very perceptive indeed."

He cannot read your mind, the voice says, which is little comfort. It takes all my will not to look at him to see if I can discern the curve of his thoughts and judge how he knows mine. He is baiting me, trying to pull me within the gravity of his power.

"You have an interesting history, Mr. Aeida," the Seeker continues, when it becomes clear that I am not going to take the hook. "Unremarkable in so many ways. You have barely made a ripple upon this world; at first we did not even notice you. But there have been some fascinating intersections that have come to light. You seem to have made a habit of coming into contact with people who do not exist here. A curious thing, that. And so we looked closer and the mysteries abound. Perhaps you can help reveal them to us."

"Why would I help you?" I ask, while I wonder what he really knows of my past, whose outlines I can barely discern. Does he know of Lasinha and Ana and our activities, or is it simply an educated guess on his part? The latter I hope.

"Why not? You don't trust this one, do you?" The Seeker points at Meredith, his disdain evident.

"No," I say, "but I don't see why I would trust you either. For all I know everything you've told me is a lie."

"I've told you nothing," the Seeker says, which I realize is more or less the truth. "While this one, no doubt, has been filling your head with ridiculous stories. An impossible universe? The very name tells you all you need to know. A universe more real than the others? How is one to determine such a thing? On what criteria is that to be judged? Faith? I think not. I will trust the science of the matter, which very much says otherwise."

"You Seekers lead such a pale life," Meredith says, her

voice filled with scorn, though she cannot hide the fear that lies beneath it. "Dissecting everything. You think in such absolute terms. There is what you know and all else is false. The universe is filled with mystery."

"Mysteries do abound," the Seeker says, never taking his eyes off me.

I swallow, nearly choking, and feel my hands begin to tremble. I stuff them in my coat pockets, to hide them from the Seeker's all-seeing gaze, and feel the cool plastic of the flashlight object on my fingertips.

Be ready.

"Do you know why you have no memory, I wonder?"

He waits for a response, the silence stretching on, his compelling presence making it an agony not to speak. "They took it from me," I say at last, and hear Meredith sigh bitterly.

"Yes, I'm sure they did," the Seeker says. "She told you that I imagine."

It is not a question, but I answer "Yes." This is dangerous territory, I know, for with each answer I give, no matter how evasive, the next will be easier for the Seeker to extract.

"It is something they are doing now," he says, making his distaste for it evident. "Barbaric really. Did she tell you why?"

Here I know the ground is too precarious to stand and refuse to venture forth. I can feel Meredith's relief, the secret safe for now. What information can I possess that the Seeker or the Society might be interested in? I assumed, and Meredith let me, that the knowledge I possess relates to the search for the impossible universe and needs to be hidden from the Seeker and the apostates like Osahi. But, if the Seeker is to be believed, they view the Church's beliefs as little more than fantasy, which suggests that whatever I know is unrelated to that. Something about the Church itself then and its members. But what?

The Seeker turns around, evidently tiring of the game he is playing. "You are both delaying the inevitable. I will find out what I want to know; it is only a matter of time. You cannot avert your eyes forever. Just as your *church* cannot maintain the pretense of being a vessel of faith for much longer.

"How many millions have been stolen from its followers to fund these little schemes of yours?" he says, glancing back at Meredith. "How much have you stolen and scavenged against all proper law in any known universe from worlds like this one? And to what end? You keep the Grand Regent in comfort, but accomplish little else."

I glance at Meredith and see her glaring at the Seeker with a wrath that frightens me. The Seeker seems not to notice, his eyes on the road ahead. We merge onto a freeway and the Black Robe driving weaves his way through the traffic with a startling ease, the cars we pass only an ill-defined blur in my window. As I struggle in vain to remember what it is I know that can be so valuable to all these people, I find myself looking at the back of the seat where the Seeker sits, his presence implacable, and I realize there is no point in trying. I will know soon enough.

31

I was alone, drinking a beer in some basement bar in downtown Vancouver, when Lasinha found me again. I had taken to coming to this place on those days when I had nothing better to do, and sometimes even on those when I did, to drink myself slowly into oblivion. To forget the need I had in me and its resulting hurt and anger. I was so powerless before Ana and she seemed so oblivious to my feelings. But not at all, I now realized, for she was awake to my longing and she was using it to manipulate me.

All the recent changes pointed to it: her attendance at the exchanges, the changes in their location, and my removal from the last one. I did not believe her concern for me was real, she was not protecting me. She had no interest in this world that I could discern. She had wanted me out of the way so she could do something. Worst of all was the hurt I felt, that she had not trusted me enough to include me in whatever plot she was carrying out. I was such an utter, pathetic fool.

Such was my mood when Lasinha leaned against the bar beside me, a crooked grin on his face. It took a moment for me to register who it was, but when I did I leapt from my seat and clapped my arms around him, clinging to him. He laughed, returning my embrace, and said, "Never good to drink alone, David Aeida. Have you lost your direction?"

I could only shrug and make a vague gesture. "Come on," he said, pointing to a booth in the corner, "I need to talk with you about something."

I nodded and followed him to the booth, sliding in opposite him. I studied his face while he ordered a drink. He seemed unchanged from the last time I had seen him, nearly two years before. That seemed strange to me. Surely I looked different, I felt so different, another person almost. He was the same as he had been, with the same ease and grace that always disarmed me. We talked for a time about where our lives had taken us since he had left, me babbling on bitterly about Ana, he being vague as always. Yet it did feel vague in the moment, it was only after, when you tried to recall the details of what he had said that you realized how little he had actually revealed.

At last I came to it, I could avoid it no more, and I said it, while I still had the courage of the beers in me. "Why did you leave?"

Here his expression changed and he became serious. "I had to. Orders from the Grand Regent. I wasn't even given time to say goodbye to anyone. I've been working on something for him, something that will change the faith itself."

"What is that?"

Lasinha smiled. He had me. "I can't say just yet. But I am guessing you would like to be a part of it?"

"Of course. I have always been faithful and served the Grand Regent."

"Yes, and don't think he has not noticed. I will make sure that you are a part of it going forward. You were always the best of my recruits here. I hated to lose you."

My heart soared hearing those words, even as I told myself not to believe him entirely. He had left without a word of goodbye and he had told me nothing so far.

His expression changed again, clouding with anger, and he said, "First, we have some work to do. You've told me a bit about the Adjudicator who replaced me, but I need to know more."

"Why?" I said.

"Because the Grand Regent has recently come to believe that some in the Church are working against him, and he suspects Ana is one of the unfaithful."

I told him everything, how I had been left to do the exchanges myself, Ana seemingly disinterested in the process, trusting me to do it, and how that had changed recently.

"She was bringing something over," I said, "and she didn't want me to see."

"Something or someone," Lasinha said grimly. "What we need to do is find out."

32

The Seeker turns his attention to me again. Though he remains facing forward, looking out absently at the freeway, I can feel his concentration shifting its locus to me, drawing me within its terrible gravity. It pulls at my thoughts, seeming to loose them from my control, compelling me to give voice to them. I resist, though I can feel the energy it costs me, and I begin to understand why the Seeker is so patient and unhurried. Both Meredith and I will break, it is inevitable. We can't resist his power forever.

That I am at war with myself doesn't help matters. Not only do I have the voice inhabiting my mind, and the memories that overwhelm me at points, there are bursts and flashes of other thoughts and emotions, like shadows in my peripheral vision. Are they other recollections? I cannot tell. They are there and then gone, yet they feel distinct from the memories that come to me whole, with scenes that feel as though I inhabited them at one time. Lasinha and Ana, I know them. These other intimations frighten me, like the voice they suggest depths that I should not contain. But what is a person's mind but a thousand contradictory and simultaneous thoughts and emotions cascading endlessly, just barely contained.

The Seeker says something to the Black Robe driving the car that I do not hear and we exit the freeway a moment later. I begin to pay attention to where we are going after that, mostly to give me something other than the Seeker to focus on, but nothing looks familiar. The city comes to an abrupt end at a townhouse-lined street, which we pass by and continue on into a forest, trees towering far above us.

The Black Robe pulls into a parking lot and the Seeker gets out and gestures to me. "Please come with me, David Aeida."

I hesitate, unsure of what to do, and glance at Meredith. She gives me a helpless look and I shrug and get out of the car. She makes to follow, but the Black Robe sitting beside her puts a hand on her shoulder.

"You may stay," the Seeker says, as though the choice is hers. "These two gentleman will give you good company. Come along, David Aeida."

I am still looking in the car at Meredith, who is frantic now as she sees that we are being separated, wondering at the cause of her agitation. Is she worried about being left alone with the Black Robes, or about what the Seeker might do to me? And what I might say to him.

The Seeker has not waited to see if I am following him and is nearly out of the parking lot and onto a path that leads into the forest. I jog to catch up with him, feeling faintly ridiculous as I do so. I have no thought of trying to escape, I know that is impossible. Strangely my fear has vanished and I realize that so has the Seeker's presence, normally so palpable. He is no longer trying to compel me to speak or peer within my thoughts.

We walk in silence, following the trail as it winds its way through the forest, and soon I can hear the rush and crash of water flowing. At first I think it is the ocean, but as we come nearer I see it was a thin and turbulent river. There is a suspension bridge stretching across the river gorge, thin and swaying as a few people make their way across it, laughing and shouting. The Seeker smiles, seemingly delighted, and leads the way onto it.

As we come to the middle, he stops and he leans over the railing, staring down at the foaming wrath of the water. I follow his lead and find myself entranced, though I cannot entirely lose myself in the moment, as I am never able to forget who is standing beside me. A few people glanced at us as they walk by, and I see a number of raised eyebrows and hushed conversations, which baffled me. This man, with his strange gray robes and his alien eyes announcing his otherworldly origins for all who wish to see it, draws no more attention than a loud argument between a couple might.

"They do not see what they do not want to see," the Seeker says. "People rarely look or listen." He has turned back to face me, and I nearly forget that I can't look in his eyes or all is lost. I turn back to study the river and so does he.

"Do you believe in fate, David Aeida?" he says.

I shrug, to say I have never considered the matter.

"You believe in free will. That your choices will define your future, and that they are yours to make."

"I suppose," I say.

"Most of us believe that," he says. "In truth I believe it. It is difficult not to. We have so many choices that we make every day, whether momentous or not. How many times did you consider whether to stay with that woman, for example. And each time you probably felt as though you could choose to stay or to go, and that the choice was yours, absent her trying to stop you. Look at your life, what little you can recall of it, and it is marked by these choices you have made. Maybe you imagine how your life might have been different, if you had done this or that, instead of some other thing. We have the appearance of an infinity of choices, just like the universes that exist.

"But it is not so. Every choice has already been

narrowed by a hundred others that you made, and the choices of millions of others, until you are left with very little to decide at all. Oh I believe in free will, just as you do. It is the human in all of us to do so. But unlike you, I can see the outlines, I know the falsity of that belief.

I nod, unsure of what to say, or whether the Seeker expects me to say anything. He smiles, turning his gaze back to the river and the tree-lined gorge. "This has been lost in my universe," he says.

"They are all different."

"Of course," the Seeker says, making an indefinable gesture with his hand. "They have to be. It cannot be otherwise. And that is why we have no free will, you understand. If every choice made has another universe where the opposite occurred, then was it really a choice? They are all you. That is why your Regents will never find their impossible universe. They will never see them all, each time they move across they create more and more. They will be searching till the end of time, and while they do they will cause irreparable damage."

I nod again. What he says makes sense, though my understanding of the many universes and how they interact and exist is hardly complete. There is so much I do not know that I have no hope of comprehending what is going on.

"What do you mean damage?" I say, only to see that he has already started across the rest of the bridge. He waits for me on the far side and I repeat my question.

"They are polluting these universes. They are not supposed to be here," the Seeker says, continuing down the trail. It descends from the gorge deeper into the rain forest, the air cool and scented with pine.

"Neither are you," I point out to him.

"I am here at the behest of the Travelers. They understand these things, how to pass back and forth without causing any ripples in the water, so to speak.

The path wanders, curving here and there, slowly

descending. We cross tributaries to the river, sparkling in the sunlight.

"Balancing things off," I say, recalling my own memories of the exchanges. I want to keep the Seeker talking, anything to forestall the moment, which I know must come, when he will peer into my soul and reveal my innermost being.

"No. That is what your Regents have never understood. When I go it will be as if I was never here. The universe will continue on as it was intended. Whereas your Regents destroy each universe they visit. It is no longer the same, and what once existed cannot be recreated."

I frown, unsure of what he is saying. This is the first time I have the sense he might be misleading me. How is what he does any different than what I did for the Church? Meredith might be able to provide an answer, though I would not trust her response. Or the voice, though it has fallen silent. I have the sense it is listening to what the Seeker has to say.

I still do not understand why the Seeker brought me here. Does he just want to tell me about fate and the universes? It seems to hardly matter, I am of no consequence to him, except as a means to get to the Church. He has no need to gain my trust as Meredith had, he doesn't need it to get what he wants. I watch him from the corner of my eye as we walk, but he seems uninterested in me for the moment.

As if sensing my thoughts, he turns and fixes his bulbous eyes on me. I am careful to keep my eyes on the path ahead, though the creeping sense of dread I felt in the car begins to return.

"You remember more than you let on, I think, David Aeida," the Seeker says. "You know of the purge in the Church, and I suspect you were involved in it in some fashion. That is not intuition on my part, by the way. It is a simple fact that the purge has consumed the entirety of the

Church. Who knows what will remain when it is through."

He speaks with authority, but I have no way of knowing the truth of what he says. None of my memories have yet touched upon the purge, or the Watchers' Order, of which I am evidently a part. This is what he wants to know, the secret that I possess. But is it what Meredith fears him discovering?

"You are their vessel, David Aeida," he continues, as we come to a pool where the water from the river gathers momentarily before rushing onward. A couple has jumped into the water just as we arrive and are screaming and laughing at the cold. "They are using you. To what end I cannot say."

"It seems everyone is using me," I says. "And telling me that only they can help me."

The Seeker laughs. "Oh, I make no secret of our intentions. You will provide us answers to the questions we have. Whether that helps you or not is of no concern to me. The Church of the Regents must be destroyed, especially now that it is fragmenting internally. This is when it is most dangerous."

"You cannot destroy belief," I say, but it is not me who says it.

"Perhaps not. We shall see," the Seeker says. "I suspect though, David Aeida, that you and I will be there in the end."

I shiver at his words, a chill of recognition cutting through me. *Be ready.* I nearly fall to my knees.

"Let us go back," the Seeker says, watching my struggles. "There is much still be done."

33

Under Lasinha's direction I began to follow Ana, observing all she did, where she went and everyone she met. Most were my fellow Regents in this universe, but there were others who seemed to have no place in the Church's workings that I could discern. Lasinha would listen to my descriptions of these encounters with great interest, asking me to describe, with as much detail as I could, what each person she met with looked like. Whatever suspicions he might have had about any of these individuals, or about Ana herself, he did not tell me. I was to observe and report, no more.

I did, of course; I would have followed wherever Lasinha led, and soon enough I did. That was not the only reason, however. I wanted to see the realization in Ana's eyes when my betrayal was made plain, wanted to see her hurt as she had wounded me. Was I so petty a person? I told myself no, accepted every justification Lasinha gave me for the actions I undertook, and yet I could never escape that terrible knowledge.

I despised myself for the pleasure I took in destroying her, my doubts that she was in fact an unbeliever only feeding my disgust in myself. Yet, no matter how much I hated myself for it, I could not stop. I never considered it.

As we grew to know her routines, we escalated our surveillance, breaking into her apartment to search it when we knew she was absent. Lasinha would have me go through every last thing, no matter how innocuous, with the greatest of care. I was never entirely sure what it was that we were looking for that would implicate her betrayal of the Grand Regent, though I soon realized it didn't matter to Lasinha. Her heresy was fact, and all that we found confirmed it, both in his eyes and the Grand Regent's. My doubts remained, but I kept them to myself, especially when evidence of a lover came to light.

He was of this world. How long had I told myself that her aversion to me was a result of her hatred of being stuck in this universe? I had deceived myself entirely. I even followed the lover, trying to see what it was he had that I lacked. It was all too much to bear in the end. I saw them together, her happier and more at ease than she had ever been in my presence. She was not the cold distant woman I knew, not at all. It was I who made her so.

At last the day arrived when Lasinha decided it was time to act. Whatever evidence of malfeasance he required we had evidently managed to gather, though I could not have said what it was. As far as I could tell, Ana was seeing to her duty as Adjudicator of this universe and no more, but Lasinha remained convinced. He had somehow gotten word that Ana would be meeting someone of import in the plot against the Grand Regent and we were to confront them both there.

I followed Ana to a sushi restaurant, where Lasinha met me. We watched from across the street as another woman, someone I did not recognize, joined her. They greeted each other warmly and sat down to order. This was the signal Lasinha was looking for, and he led me into the restaurant, heading directly to their table to confront them.

"I'm afraid your ruse is over," Lasinha said to them. "You'll both have to come with me."

"On whose authority?" Ana said, her cheeks going red with anger. The other woman barely stirred, her expression blank, though her eyes were watchful.

"Whose do you think?" Lasinha said, this time looking at the other woman as he showed them both a signet.

At the sight of it, Ana's face went white, but still she did not back down. "I am here under the Church's authority. This universe is my domain by their edict."

"His authority is the Church's authority. You know that as well as I," Lasinha said. "No matter how much some might like to see it changed."

"Only an edict from the Church itself can overrule my jurisdiction here," Ana said, clenching her hands, her fury barely contained. I felt sick watching her, bitter with the knowledge of what was to come, of the fire that would be extinguished. If only, I thought, but such doubts would not be allowed me for much longer.

"That is no longer the case," Lasinha said, "as you will soon see. The Grand Regent has issued a new edict and created a new jurisdiction beyond the purview of the High Regents and the Adjudicators. We are to investigate heresy and we are free to go wherever we please to find it. We answer to him alone."

Ana looked as though she were about to argue further, but the woman with her stood up, shaking her head. "There's no use. He will have his way."

Lasinha nodded, glad that someone was willing to see reason, and gestured for Ana to rise, which she did only after a long pause.

"I expected better of you," she said to me in a numb voice. I offered no reply, leading her out of the restaurant by the arm, Lasinha taking the other woman with him.

We sent them back across to the other universe that night. Lasinha did not tell me what became of Ana or the other woman and I did not ask, desperately wanting to know, and yet fearing the answer. In the end I knew, though, I knew what was going to happen to her after crossing over. I could see it in her eyes, hear it in her voice. *I expected better of you.* My heart ached each time I heard it again in my thoughts.

34

We return to the car where Meredith and Black Robes await us in uncomfortable silence. Meredith seeks out my eyes urgently, trying to discern from them what happened in my time alone with the Seeker. I don't look at her, my thoughts turning to the interrogation to come. It seems apparent that I will be made to answer for crimes I have no memory of committing.

You must escape now, or you never will, the voice says. If I understand what the Seeker told me, he can hold me prisoner indefinitely while he exacts whatever punishment he has in mind and forces me to answer whatever questions he may have.

That is not a thought I relish, and as the Black Robe takes us from the forest back into the city, my hand strays for my jacket pocket. I find the object hidden there and I decided to see whether it is of any use at all. I carefully run my fingers along its smooth length, until I find what I think is a button and shift it so that neither end is pointing at me. Though I would feel far more comfortable if I could take it from my jacket, I don't dare give either the Seeker, or the Black Robe sitting beside me, time to act. For all I know I might be putting myself in far greater danger than I already am, but the voice is silent and I take that as consent for what I am about to do, and press the button.

It locks when I depress it fully and begins to emit an almost imperceptible whine as I go stiff with fear. The sound continues for several seconds, moments that stretch endlessly for me as I silently entreat it to do whatever it is going to do before I am found out. No one else in the car seems to hear the sound, and I begin to worry that the object is not a weapon, as the voice clearly believes. I have to resist the urge to take it out and inspect it.

Brace yourself.

At the same moment as that thought emerges, urgent and clear, the Seeker whirls around in his seat, the mask gone from his features. "What have you done?"

I don't answer, but our eyes meet for the briefest of seconds and I feel again as though he sees all of me that there is. Before either of us has time to react, the whine of the object ceases, and is followed by what sounds to me like a gasp for air after a punch to the stomach. I close my eyes, turning my face away, by instinct, warding off an invisible blow.

No other sound comes, and the object feels inert in my hands, but when I open my eyes I see that everyone else in the car is unconscious. Before I have time to fully process that, to say nothing of the fact that the car is still going forward without a driver, something makes me glance out the window and I see that everyone on the sidewalk of the street we are on has collapsed to the ground. There is a loud crash behind us as two cars careen into each other. That brings me back to myself, and I turn back in time to see the car in front of us veer off into a parked car, its back end jutting out and blocking our path. The words of the voice return to me and I brace myself.

35

The woman was staring at me. She had unsettling eyes, green and elusive, light as quicksilver, questioning me. She was taking my measure. They both were. I shuffled on my feet, uneasy, meeting her gaze, only because to meet his was more than I could bear. Sensing my discomfort, she allowed a hint of a smile to play across her lips, moving a possessive hand to his shoulder. Her touch seemed to stir him from his own contemplation of me and he looked over to Lasinha, who stood at my side.

"This is the David Aeida of whom you have spoken," the Grand Regent said, his tone suggesting that I in no way matched the tales Lasinha had been telling.

"Yes, Grand Regent," Lasinha said, always eager to persuade. "As I said, he has been a loyal servant to the Church and to you. He was instrumental in my work in the Fifty-Ninth universe and proved himself again when I returned to deal with the heresy of the Adjudicator."

"So you say," the Grand Regent said. He did not seem convinced.

I was not convinced myself. The Grand Regent was not dressed as I would have expected. He was wearing a fine, but ordinary suit. I had expected a papal uniform or some sort of officious ostentation that would mark him as a leader of the faith. It was his eyes, though, that compelled, that drew me in.

Lasinha wet his lips. "He has been a faithful and unquestioning servant," he said, emphasizing the latter. "Faith is his one true guiding force."

The Grand Regent returned his gaze to me and again I could not meet his terrible eyes, fearsome and devoid of emotion, as was his voice, which rang out through the room. "Is this true?" he said.

I forced myself to look at him and nodded. "Yes. I am committed to this faith and I will sacrifice anything to find the impossible world."

The Grand Regent nodded and glanced at the woman at his side. He had the angular features of an Eastern European, though he possessed no discernable accent. She was unplaceable, both by look and by her expressions.

"Words are easy. Faith must be demonstrated through deed and sacrifice. What are you willing to sacrifice, sub-Regent?"

"Everything. Anything," I said, though I was unsure as I said it, not knowing what he wanted me to say and desperate that he should hear it and that the interrogation should end.

The Grand Regent noticed my irresolution and smiled. "I ask of all my faithful only what I ask of myself. Do you understand? If we are to triumph over the forces arrayed against us, both without and, sadly, within this Church, we must remain committed. Our faith must be absolute. There can be no room for doubt or prevarication. Since my revelation, I have given all that I am and all that I will be to the True Faith. The Lieutenant was my guide, as he is to us all, but I worked directly in his shadow and so was nourished, as fungus flourishes in darkness. He chose me to continue his work when his sub-carcass left him unable to continue, and I have, never forgetting all that he taught me. Not just in his writings and sayings, all of which I'm sure you are familiar with, but in all that he shared with me in our too brief time together."

He stood, warming to his speech, the words coursing out of him. Here at last was his emotion, but it still seemed abstract, unattached to any real feeling. The substance of him was missing and within lay a swirling void that I could almost perceive in his eyes. It was entrancing, both drawing me and repelling me. I had to look away, returning my gaze to the woman who had her own allure. There was something familiar about her, a twitch of memory that I could not quite place.

"I have absorbed all his teachings, as he absorbed the secret missives of the higher ones who blessed him with their sacred knowledge from which we draw all our power. Never forget it all flows from De Gofroy. But how could you? His teaching imbues us all. It inhabits us, as we inhabit these vessels, our secondary carcasses."

The Grand Regent paused in his recitation, for it was clear to me that he had said these very words to many others before me, in rooms very much like this one, in other universes to others like me. Had Lasinha recruited then as well? He had been busy since he left my world to Ana. The Grand Regent trusted him, that much was evident at least, or he would not have risked crossing over merely to see me, a sub-Regent of no consequence. I wanted desperately to turn to Lasinha for reassurance, or to look to the strange woman who had accompanied the Grand Regent on his journey. What was her place here? Was she the Grand Regent's lover, his protector? I could not tell. But I dared not turn away from the man himself, for it was clear that this was the decisive moment where I was to be judged. I could not be found lacking, not after what I had done.

"But my mind strays from the task at hand. It is a poor habit, I am afraid, that others are always counseling me against." Here he turned to the woman and smiled. Lovers, then, I decided, though by the way she stood behind him, looking past me, alert to the sounds of the rooms around us, she might be his guard as well.

"Just as I am the Lieutenant's vessel, and we all are the vessels of our true, first selves, you seek to become my vessel, to be directed by my hand alone. The Church has entered a precarious moment. You cannot begin to understand the danger we are in. The Society of Travelers, those perverse guardians of the false order of the universes, have made it their task to destroy us. They have placed agents throughout the Church, seedlings that they hope will grow long enough stalks to bear poisoned fruit.

"And so they have," he said, becoming grave and still for a moment, as though mourning the betrayals he had been faced with. "The situation has become so precarious that I cannot even trust my most holiest of servants, the High Regents and the Adjudicators. Where to turn, then? I look to my old friend Lasinha, who stood beside me in my time of revelation and who has guided many more along that true and sacred path. You owe him your faith. Together we will find people such as yourself, unpolluted by the intrigues that plague our Church, to stand watch against the false amongst us. We need people of ambition, discretion, and absolute fealty. Lasinha tells me you are one such person."

He paused, and I realized he expected me to say something. "That is for you to judge, Grand Regent. I desire only to be your servant."

The Grand Regent smiled as though I had passed some grave test, and I felt a bit of tension begin to leech from my sinews. "Welcome to the Watchers' Order, David Aeida," he said. "I feel confident you will make a fine vessel."

He nodded at Lasinha, who bowed in turn, thanking him for accepting me into his service. "He will not disappoint."

The Grand Regent launched into another speech on the perfidy of the Society and the threats arrayed against the One Faith, of which we were the last remaining guardians, and I seized the opportunity to steal another glance at the woman who had accompanied him. She was watching me as well, and our eyes met briefly, my face going flush under her scrutiny. Unlike the Grand Regent, who had looked through me, attempting merely to intimidate, and succeeding, she was actually taking the measure of me, wanting to judge my reactions now that I had been inducted into her Order. What she was thinking I could not tell, but I noticed that her face had none of the glowing fealty that Lasinha's did when the Grand Regent looked upon her.

What it all meant, I could not begin to guess. There were too many hidden alliances, even among the four of us in this room, that I could not begin to make sense of whatever larger picture lay beyond this room and this universe. Would I ever, or would it be my lot to toil in ignorance, sacrificing for the greater cause?

My thoughts, and the Grand Regent's speech, were interrupted by a knock at the door, and another woman slipped in, looking from face to face, though I rated only the barest of glances. "Are you finished?" she said without preamble.

The Grand Regent smiled at her words, the indulgent patron. "Yes, we are. I suppose you think we should be going?"

"It's dangerous to stay longer than necessary," she said.

"Of course," he said, his smile widening. He nodded to Lasinha and the three of them left, only the Grand Regent's companion giving me a sidelong glance on her way out.

That was not what stayed with me in the days that followed as I relived each moment of that singular encounter. It was the moment right after the Grand Regent had agreed to leave, as he looked upon the woman who had entered with a longing and a possessiveness he could not hide. It was there for an instant and then gone.

More significant, though, was what followed, as the two women shared a glance. The Grand Regent's companion I could not read; she remained a cipher. The newcomer, though, her emotions were written as plainly on her face as the Grand Regent's had been, jealousy, hatred, and desire all intermingling.

Were we all so naked, stripped bare to our cores in these moments when we were not even aware of ourselves? Is that how Lasinha had known to use me against Ana, trusting that my unrequited desire would fester into a thirst for vengeance?

The memory of it all swam through me, the images repeating. The Grand Regent, his companion, and the interloper and their shared and broken moment. The woman who had entered I knew from somewhere, it occurred to me, a distant thought, as though I were slipping from the holds of a dream into wakefulness. It was Meredith.

36

I taste blood in my mouth as I come back to myself, blinking and fighting at the darkness that threatens to send me under again. It takes me several moments to realize where I am. The car, the Seeker, everyone else on the street, all appear to have gone still. My whole body aches from the aftermath of the collision. I check myself for broken bones, but I seem more or less in one piece.

Gingerly reaching across the Black Robe, terrified that I might somehow jar him awake, I shake Meredith, trying to see if I can rouse her. She does not respond. The effort is so agonizing I groan aloud. The darkness swims to the surface of my vision again and I have to breath deeply several times before I am able to force it aside.

Run.

I ignore the voice, shaking Meredith again, even daring to whisper her name. She does not stir, and I blink back tears from the pain of my efforts.

Run. Leave her. Now.

I fumble at the door, but it is locked. I have to reach in front of me, to where the Seeker lies, mercifully still unconscious, and press the door locks, releasing me. Every movement, every sound—the thunk of the doors being unlocked especially—is marked by fear that this will be the thing that starts everyone back to consciousness. It does not happen, and I open my door and slip out, moving in a painstaking fashion, not even daring to close the door behind me.

Run. Run.

I waver, dizzy on my feet, and when I regain my equilibrium I go around to the other side of the car, ignoring the frantic demands of the voice, and open the door, pulling Meredith out. Her body is still limp and I struggle clumsily with it, spilling her to the ground. Crouching over her, I somehow manage to pick her up, cradling her in my arms, although my entire body protests, the agony so severe it drowns out the voice.

I stumble forward, quickly realizing that it is beyond my capabilities to go any distance, especially with Meredith in my arms. Ahead I can see a car that drifted to a stop against another, undamaged and still idling, the driver having taken her foot off the gas when she lost consciousness. I go to it and somehow maneuver the woman out of the car and Meredith into the front passenger seat. The effort leaves me exhausted and aching, my whole body trembling.

In the distance I hear sirens, and I know I do not have time gather myself. With shaking hands, I shift the car into reverse and begin to maneuver it out of the traffic jam I created. The flashing lights of the first responders to the accident are just visible in my rearview mirror as I escape the tangle of cars on the street and speed away, ignoring the stares of the growing number of bystanders.

FIVE:

LAILA

37

I have no idea how long I've been driving or where I've gone. The city spreads out around me, the streets all looking much the same as anywhere, lined with houses here, apartment buildings and storefronts there, the steady grid unchanging for the most part. The streets all seem to be numbered: 152 Street, 85 Avenue. Neighborhoods have names but I don't recognize any of them. Beside me Meredith remains unconscious, though I can hear her breathing, soft but steady, reassuring me that she is not seriously hurt from the weapon discharge. I threw it out the window at some point in my journey, thinking it might give the Seeker an easier means of tracking me. He certainly didn't require any of my help.

Though my journey feels aimless, I do seem to be heading generally south and east, the city gradually giving way to fields, bits of forest, and sloughs, as well as massive greenhouses and acreages. Soon I am on a two-lane highway, largely empty of traffic, with signs pointing to Mission and Abbotsford, Chilliwack and Vernon. The names are familiar and foreign at the same time. I am certain I have heard of them before, but I have no sense of what they might be like or if I should go to them. Can I just continue driving, off across the country, forever outrunning the Seeker?

My instincts say no, and instead I find myself turning onto a side road that soon narrows and runs out of pavement, turning to gravel. Surrounding me are fields lined with fruit trees and corn, with only the odd house and yard to be seen, usually surrounded by a wall of trees that hide most of what is within from sight. As I go, I have the distinct sensation that I have traveled these roads before, though no memories emerge to corroborate the feeling, and as I come to intersection after intersection I unerringly chose a direction until I come to a dead end road—more a laneway that curves into a small valley— passing a few farms on either side and ending at a small farmhouse.

The yard is cluttered and unkempt, filled with tall grass and thick with weeds gone to seed, surrounded by a thick row of trees that obscures it from the road. The house is set atop a small rise within the valley, giving it the appearance of being surrounded by a moat of grass. A thin trail leads from the lane, going between the wall of trees, around to the back of the house. I follow it, pulling to a halt and getting out of the car.

Quiet reigns, the only sounds the breeze stirring the grass and the branches in the trees, along with the chatter of birds and insects. The world seems still and poised, waiting for something that will disturb this idyll. I wait too, for the Seeker to appear, or Meredith to rouse herself, or the secrets that lie within me to emerge.

38

The next time I saw the Grand Regent he was alone, unaccompanied by Meredith or the strange woman. Lasinha had crossed over to another universe, as far as I knew, so I was left to alone to complete my duties, which consisted mostly of observing the other Regents operating in this world. All of us were natives to this universe, by and large centered in Vancouver and other cities along the west coast, where Lasinha had focused most of his energies, though we sometimes had to travel to Nigeria and Ukraine, where he had others working. Another Adjudicator had been sent across to replace Ana, and we spent a great deal of time ensuring she was acting in accordance with the protocols of the Church, of which I had become something of an expert by this point.

Everyone had become suspect in Lasinha's eyes. Never mind that most of the native faithful had neither the knowledge nor the skills to betray the Church; I was to observe them closely to ensure that they remained true at heart to the faith. I became an expert at disappearing into the background; even those who knew me from the early days with Lasinha failed to notice me watching and listening to them. My absence from my regular church meetings was easily explained—people came and went from the faith all the time, and my unrequited desire for Ana had been, much to my embarrassment, well known, providing a useful reason should I have a chance run-in with someone. I never did; our lives were too separate and I was far too careful.

I took to my new life with ease, seduced by the allure of the secrets that were now mine, as well as the power to unmake lives I now possessed. It was only too easy to salve my guilt over what I had done to Ana by giving myself to Lasinha and the Watchers fully. That we had a seemingly unlimited means to achieve our aims did not hurt matters. I was no longer living a life of sacrifice and denial. I was the possessor of the arcane and the untold wealth that apparently came with it.

I was preparing for a flight to Las Vegas where a half-dozen Regents were located when the Grand Regent entered my apartment, somehow bypassing the lock without my hearing it. How long he observed me without my realizing he was there I cannot say, but I only became aware of his presence when he spoke, a sudden voice behind where I sat in my living room, going over my luggage.

"Are you still a faithful vessel, David Aeida?"

His voice, emotionless and precise, sent chills down my spine. "I remain your servant," I said, resisting the urge to turn around and look at him, sensing that it would somehow be a mistake to do so.

There was a long pause as he considered my reply before he made his way around and sat across from me on the couch. He was dressed as a native of this world, unlike the last time I had seen him, when he had been wearing a scarlet coat and suit, as though he were an eighteenth century dandy. He still looked incongruous perched among my possessions, his otherworldliness apparent even in disguise. I waited for him to speak again, wondering what had brought the Grand Regent to me, tendrils of fear curling in my stomach as various possibilities presented themselves to me.

"I am happy to hear it, David," the Grand Regent said at last. I had passed whatever test he had submitted me to. "The forces arrayed against us grow bolder and more varied by the day, I am afraid to say. And at a time when it becomes ever more important that we be united, our Church grows ever more divided. The result, I am sorry to say, of Society agents, among others, working to sow divisions amongst the faithful. That they have been successful only demonstrates the frailty of our beings, the core nature of our vesseldom."

He paused in his oration to look at me and I nodded, for I felt it was expected of me. I knew nothing really of the struggles he referred to; I knew nothing of the other universes beyond what Lasinha had told me, and that was very little. But I had seen little evidence in all my surveillance of my fellow Regents to indicate that any of the divisions or plots that Lasinha and the Grand Regent saw amongst the faithful existed. I kept my doubts to myself, though, for my part in it all was insignificant and my view of the Church was obviously but a small piece. Perversely, though, as with Ana, my doubts about what I was doing only served to affirm my faith with the cause, to commit myself to it fully. I could not explain it, yet it was so. Was it this aspect of my nature that drew Lasinha, and now the Grand Regent, to me?

"What have you seen of Lasinha?" the Grand Regent asked, interrupting my thoughts.

"What do you mean?" I said, unable to keep the disbelief from my voice.

"Are you so surprised?" he said, giving me a distant smile. "I institute the Watchers' Order to bring these outside agents to light, and yet they continue to flourish. Evil reigns. One has to question if Lasinha is doing his job adequately or if he is allowing these things to fester until the limb has to be removed."

This was another test, I thought, as fear clenched my chest like a vise. A test of what, though? My loyalty to Lasinha? The Church? The Grand Regent? I did not know, but it seemed certain that my fate, and perhaps Lasinha's, hinged upon my answer.

"I know only what I see of him," I said, "and it seems to me he is a loyal servant to the True Faith, as we all are. Is it not through his efforts that all this has come to light? Are you not better for knowing this?"

The Grand Regent leaned back on the couch, looking very tired, the force that had animated him draining away. He sighed. "Perhaps you are correct. Lasinha has been with me from the beginning and has proven himself true at every turn. As have you to him, David Aeida. Your loyalty to him is a credit to you."

I nodded my thanks, not daring to say more.

"The times are faulty, I am afraid," he continued, looking past me now. "I had been so certain that it would be mine to find the impossible world, to reunite us with our true forms, that we might transcend these poor vessels. Now that day seems more distant than when I first stepped into De Gofroy's embrace. How is such a thing possible?"

It was not a question that I could answer, nor did he seem to expect me to.

"Do you know," he said, the emotion in his voice taking me aback, "what it is like to be betrayed by those closest to you? Those that you have loved and given everything to? Nothing can mend the wound. Nothing."

Here, I thought, was the real man hidden behind the Grand Regent. His anger was terrifying to witness, for it did not explode as with so many people, but was quiet and sinister, with the promise of violence. Had he spoken this way to Ana after I sent her across to face her judgment? The thought horrified me.

Abruptly the Grand Regent stood up, his face composed, and the fury and despair that had briefly marked his eyes vanished. "I thank you, David Aeida, for your clarifying words on my friend Lasinha. You have set my mind to ease."

"I am happy to serve the faith," I said, bowing my head.

"That is good. You are fine vessel for it. A fine vessel," he said, musing to himself.

I could see the moment the thought reached its conclusion and he turned his gaze back to me, his eyes intent on mine. "I fear I will have further need of you in the days to come, David Aeida. Great need. It may be that I shall have to disappear for a time. My enemies grow too close and they know too much. Evil lurks. There are things to be done and they shall have to answer. In the meantime, though, in the meantime…"

He appeared about to say more but stopped, nodding to himself before smiling at me. "We shall have cause to speak again, David Aeida."

I nodded, unable to summon any reply, aware that this was the greatest honor I had ever received in my life, yet unable to shake the dread that filled my thoughts.

39

I see no movement within the house, but I wait some time to allow anyone who might be inside the opportunity to come out and greet me. Meredith remains unchanged, and I leave her in the car, being sure to take the keys with me, as I make a circuit around the yard, wading through the thick grass, to see if there is anything I missed from the car as I passed by. There is nothing, and at last, being unable to avoid it any longer, I go to the door and knock.

"Hello," I call out, feeling a deep and inexplicable trepidation.

There is no response and I try again, rapping so hard on the door my knuckles hurt. The door is unlocked when I try it, and I step within, calling out again, "Sorry, I'm lost. Is there anyone here?"

It smells empty, heavy with dust and stale air. I leave the door open to let some fresh air in and make my way from the landing down the short and narrow hallway to the kitchen. This is the rear entrance to the house, obviously, for there is a laundry and coatroom off to the side of the landing, a new addition, by the look of it. The kitchen is bare, an empty table with three chairs, and the only thing on the counters are a drying rack, a cutting board, and a knife holder with a few knives. I open a few cupboards, finding only a few odds and ends of dishes and a few cans of beans of indeterminate age.

From there I go to the living room, which is also sparsely furnished, a couch and a few chairs with a coffee table in the center of the room. No television or stereo. There is a broad bay window that looks out on the front yard. I can just make out the road through the trees. I sit on the couch, watching the wind move the tangle of grass outside, absorbing the silence. A bird, tiny with wings blurring, flits across the window, alighting briefly on the ledge at various points, never long enough that its wings go still. A body in perpetual motion.

I have been here before, I am certain of it. The memory refuses to stir from the absence, that black, gaping space that continues to defy me. The voice has gone silent, disappearing for all I can tell. Its absence, after so long, frightens me. What is happening to me? It seems I am a dozen people at once, all these conflicting flashes of memory, clattering around, bursting free at any given moment, the voice shouting over them. My own thoughts are not my own.

I am David Aeida. Those memories are the strongest, they come to me whole, with a clarity that none of my other thoughts have. My guilt over Ana, my loyalty toward Lasinha, the fear and mistrust I feel for the Grand Regent. Those are all tangible things; I feel them as I felt them at the moment they occurred. Why, then, do they feel like someone else's memories? Why does this body feel so wrong?

My revulsion for it is overwhelming. Sometimes I can hold it at bay and not think about it, especially when I am under threat and being assaulted by so many contrary thoughts. But now, in these slow moments, where the universe seems to pause in its mad, spinning scramble, it is all I can do not to scratch at my arms and try to tear the skin from them. My breath rasps in my throat and I think of the knives sitting in the holder on the kitchen counter. I imagine taking one and peeling off my skin, layer by layer, until I am free of the hold this flesh had upon me.

My hands shake as I imagine the knife in them, and I close my eyes, trying to will myself to stay where I am. "I am David Aeida," I say, again and again as I choke back sobs.

When I open my eyes, blinking at the sting of tears, Meredith stands above me. She has a hand on her head as though it aches and a puzzled, distant expression in her eyes. She is looking out the window at the yard, the sun upon her face, which is luminous in its gentle light. My breath goes still at her beauty, as though it has just been unveiled to me. The curve of her lips, the gleaming blue of her eyes, and the strands of hair that leap free from her carefully pulled-back hair. The playfulness that lies just beneath the surface of her careful reserve. All of it is new, or perhaps remembered now.

Meredith turns from whatever it is she was gazing at and notices the look on my face. She smiles and something like electricity scatters across my body, surging. "Thank you for saving me from the Seeker," she says.

I shrug as if there was nothing else I could have done.

"I would have been lost without you. I can never repay you for that," she says.

I struggle to find something to say again, and she bends down, pressing her warm lips against my own, her hands upon my shoulders. For a moment I go still, fear and revulsion eating at me, but only for a moment, and then I surrender to her embrace.

40

The Grand Regent and the woman sat watching each other, through low-lidded eyes, from across a small table in a room that I somehow knew lay within the Grand Regent's chambers. Layers of mistrust, of shared history and betrayal, lay between them. I could sense it, even from where I sat.

I was not there, the realization came next, almost thrusting me from the memory. I had no locus in this place, my perspective moving about as though I were watching a film instead of trapped in my memory. But whose memory was it?

The woman, whose name still refused to emerge from the depths of my mind, seemed wary of the Grand Regent, as though expecting an outburst of emotion. He was a simple enough man to read, though no less intimidating for it, his emotion always cresting above the surface of his visage. Yet his rages would still catch people unaware, a loud burst of emotion calculated to keep others off guard. It made him seem mad, unpredictable, and perhaps he was.

There was an emptiness at the center of his charisma, one I had noticed from the first as well, that left an uneasy taste after the flush of attraction and emotion had washed away. He inspired loyalty and faith, asked for and received complete obedience from his flock. He commanded, and we were thankful for his guidance. De Gofroy, he claimed, spoke through him. Perhaps it was so. But the emptiness was always there, visible, drawing us in further. Was there anything behind the well-turned phrases, his seeming ability to understand our deepest hopes and fears? Was our faith well placed?

There was something of my relationship with Lasinha in the woman's relationship with the Grand Regent, I could see. He had been there at the beginning for her, bringing her further into his orbit as he rose through the Church's hierarchy. Her faith in De Gofroy's protocols, in the search for the impossible world, the one true universe, were fundamentally tied to him.

And, of course, their relationship had been much more, anyone could see that to look at them.

"What are you thinking about?" he said, bringing a smile to his lips.

She smiled as well, though it was more guarded. "It's what I am trying not to think about."

"You're still worried about what we are doing?" he said. "I understand. It left me uncomfortable at first as well, when the Acolytes came to me with their ideas. But it must be done. There are enemies in our midst. You know that better than I. Evil must be met with force; we cannot quiver and hide from it. The future of the Church, of all its work, is at stake. The Travelers will see us ruined."

She did not reply. It felt like a discussion they had had many times before, the Grand Regent's answers rote yet insistent. He wanted her to understand. It was important, no matter that the decision had been made, and that it was his to make, he needed her to see why. The necessity of it consumed him, touching all his thoughts, and it wounded him that she did not share in this understanding.

His wife. The realization again almost shook me from the memory, my own thoughts resurfacing, the vision clouding before coming into focus again.

"I can see you're troubled by this," he said, taking her hands into his. "But you know that I need you, now more than ever. Your faith has always been a light to me. You have been a fine vessel. A true vessel in these faulty times. My secrets are yours."

He did not trust her anymore, I thought. She felt it too. There was a change, a slight dimming, to her eyes as she returned his gaze and smile.

"I must speak with Lasinha today," he said, rising to his feet as there was a knock at the door.

"You trust him," she said, as though she did not.

"He has been with us from the beginning," the Grand Regent said.

"We've always served the faith in our ways."

"Yes," he said, giving her another smile. This one, though, was distant, almost abstract.

He went to the door, admitting Meredith to the room. They shared a glance, freighted with emotion, they believed the woman did not notice.

"You know Meredith, of course," the Grand Regent said.

She did.

41

Meredith is watching me as I awake, head propped up on her arm, as she lies beside me. She smiles at me and I force one in return, though my insides rebel against it. I think of what we did last night, of her naked body beside my own, and I worry I will be sick right there. My flesh seems in rebellion against me. This is not my body. I can feel my hands start to tremble.

I close my eyes to calm myself, and when I open them Meredith leans across to kiss me, her breath warm in my mouth and her lips with a taste that can only be hers. She runs her hand down my side, coming to rest on my hip, and I am unable to stop myself from shuddering.

"Something wrong?" she says, looking concerned.

"No," I say, putting my hand over hers and squeezing it. "Just geese flying over my grave."

"What an odd thing to say," she says, giving me a look.

"People say it here. It's a thing."

"How are you feeling?" she says. "You were having trouble at the compound. It seemed like you were falling apart. Were you remembering things?"

"Yes," I say. "I think so. I'm not sure exactly. It seems to have stopped now."

There is some truth in all of that, enough that I almost believe myself and Meredith seems to accept it easily enough. The voice at least has gone silent, even as my memories as David Aeida continue to flow to the surface, disjointed and half formed. A strange and confusing sensation, as bewildering as this body that does not feel my own. I am David Aeida.

But am I? How am I to reconcile what I know to be true, the one thing I can cling to as real, with this latest memory? It is not my own, that much seems clear, unless I somehow pieced it together from a story told me. It feels like all the other memories though, real and vivid, filled with detail that has the weight of reality, not the lightness of a vision that might evaporate at a touch.

Whose memory is it? It has to be either the Grand Regent's or the woman's. Why can I not remember her name, is that somehow significant? The idea of there being more than just me within my head makes a kind of sense, given all the dislocation in my thoughts. All those flashes, those thoughts that never quite form, are they mine or someone else's? It doesn't seem possible that two people can exist in one head, but the existence of other universes seemed impossible as well, and I have no reason to doubt them now.

Sensing Meredith watching me again, I sigh and roll onto my back. "How long do we have before the Seeker is after us again?"

She slides in close to me, her fingers playing with the hairs upon my chest. I can feel her breasts pressing against me and feel something stir within me, though my revulsion remains. It feels wrong. It all feels wrong.

"A few days, I would guess. They will have had to cross over. And they might think twice about sending a Seeker over again. I would guess the police will be looking for them. And it'll be all over the news. It could be very good for us."

"They seemed to move about pretty openly."

"Yes. People see what they want to see, most of the time. It's easy to dismiss or rationalize, but not after you triggered the pulse, and especially not after they disappeared. They've drawn way too much attention. And attention is the last thing the Society wants in an untouched universe."

"We're untouched, are we?"

"Supposed to be," Meredith says with a grin, kissing my cheek. The veneer she has maintained since our meeting the coffee shop is completely gone now. She is herself, only more so, alight and free.

I allow my thoughts to drift away, trying to quell the warring desires thrashing beneath the surface. If the Seeker is gone, at least for now, I have time to let my memory return, as it seems to be doing, especially now that I am free of the compound and the suppressants. There are things I need to investigate as well, starting with this house and what connection I have to it. I am unsure whether Meredith recognizes it or not, but I suspect she did. She is another thing that I need to sort out; my feelings and desires are suddenly so confused on the matter, and yet I know I cannot trust her. The embrace still strikes like a blow.

"So," I say in a tentative voice, "what do we do now?"

Meredith laughs and rolls atop me, her lips seizing mine, as she gives me her answer.

42

I moved into Lasinha's compound amidst the mountains of West Vancouver that winter. It had become the epicenter of the Order's work in all the universes, and he wanted me at hand to oversee its operations when he was not present. It was a mansion of almost unbelievable luxury, the sort tax exiles from Hong Kong would inhabit, which the Order had expanded massively, at considerable cost, excavating deep within the mountain. There were rooms for interrogation, holding cells for those in transit, as well as equipment and technology that I did not have any idea about.

All the material that Lasinha and I had used to smuggle out of the universe now passed through the compound, for the Order's use. The rest of the faithful in our world had no sense that any change in the hierarchy had taken place, for Lasinha had worked very hard to see that someone obedient was in place as an adjudicator, and of course he and I were there to ensure that everything was done to our liking.

Hundreds of people passed through the compound as well, from all sorts of universes. Some of them were Watchers, here to be debriefed by Lasinha or myself. Some were under suspicion, brought in for questioning to see that they still properly adhered to the protocols of the faith. The Grand Regent himself often called upon us, though only when Lasinha was present. He was always accompanied by Meredith, whom Lasinha told me was his most trusted assistant. Though she was slight of build, there was something of a threat to her, and I was quite certain that she was capable of violence if the situation called for it.

The woman came only infrequently. The wife of the Grand Regent. I never did get her name. As uncomfortable as I was in the presence of the Grand Regent, I was doubly so when she was there. It seemed as though she could see deep within my thoughts, and unlike almost anyone else I had ever encountered I could read nothing of her own mind. I don't know why, but I found the void that she presented to be terrifying and, as a result, I did not trust her.

Her relationship with the Grand Regent seemed strange to me, especially once I was told that she was his wife. There was no warmth between them, no familiarity about them. They were like strangers when they touched. In fact, the more I watched them, the more certain I became that the Grand Regent was sleeping with Meredith. There was affection there, shared in glances when they thought no one was looking. Real emotion as well, not all of it warm, for sometimes I would catch Meredith looking at the Grand Regent with undisguised hatred. Did she wish the woman gone from the scene, and herself raised to her position?

I had only been in the compound a month or two, perhaps more, managing to settle into the routine of my new duties, when I saw Ana again. She was in one of the chambers on the second floor whose purpose I was unaware of, though it contained what looked like an operating table and some other medical-looking equipment. This was the domain of the Acolytes, and I generally avoided it if I could, knowing my presence would only arouse questions from Lasinha and the Grand Regent. That was the last thing I wanted in my present position at the fulcrum of the Order's work, to say nothing of the fact that the rooms and the Acolytes who worked them left me cold, with an unease that I could not explain, the dull flicker of a lost memory.

Lasinha had sent me to get a message from the Acolyte on one of the Regents they were monitoring, and when I arrived at the chamber in question I found the room empty but for Ana perched uncomfortably on the operating table. She looked up expectantly at my entrance, but there was no trace of recognition in her eyes when she saw me.

"Ana," I said in disbelief, and she smiled involuntarily, still giving no sign that she knew who I was.

"Yes," she said. "Do I need my procedure?"

I shuddered at the word. I had assumed she had been imprisoned by the Order, or cast out and left for the Society to do with her as they would. Murdered, even, in my bleakest, most fearful moments. This seemed infinitely worse, though.

I walked toward her, letting the door seal behind me, and peered intently into her beautiful eyes. She was expressionless under my examination, blank and accepting of my authority. It seemed impossible to breathe.

"Don't you remember me?" I said at last, whispering the words, not wanting to hear them myself. She frowned and studied me, ever obedient, and shook her head. She hesitated, about to speak, and a cloud passed across her expression, and she blinked, confused and fearful.

I reached out to put a comforting hand on her shoulder, and was about to say something more, when the door opened behind me and the Acolyte entered the chamber.

"What are you doing?" she said to me. I turned and faced her, open-mouthed. "You are not to interact with her. She is rejecting the tamp and the suppressants are wearing off."

I stared at the Acolyte dumbfounded, the words not quite seeming to make sense. Ana looked as confused as I, touching her face, a look of horror beginning to form. Noticing it, the Acolyte seized me by the arm and dragged me to the door. "Get out. Now."

"You have a message for Lasinha," I managed to say as I was shoved out the door, trying and failing to make it sound like a command.

"I've given it to you," the Acolyte said, already turning away from me and starting back toward Ana.

I watched her back, which hid Ana from view, until the door closed and they were both lost to my sight. The hallway was empty and soundless and I remained, rooted where I was, my thoughts lost to me. The horror that had begun to cross Ana's face seized me as well. Had I been in these rooms before? Before the sensation could overwhelm, I fled the corridor, returning to find Lasinha and deliver the Acolyte's message.

43

We spend days in bed, only rising when hunger chases us out, to feast upon a can of beans or watery pasta, with tins of fruit for dessert. Meredith sleeps often, seemingly still feeling the effects of the pulse discharge, but each time she awakes she is ravenous with need. I track the time while she sleeps by watching the changing shadows in the room and the angle of the sun that slants through the window.

After a time my desire and revulsion wear away, leaving only my raw flesh and her supple touch. It all feels so familiar, each movement a part of a greater symphony we have played so many times before, and will continue to play throughout the night and into the next day until the perfection we desire has been achieved. Until then need still remains, perhaps never to be sated.

Silence reigns during the interludes between our exertions, neither of us wanting to disturb the ecstatic peace between us. At one juncture, as Meredith traces the line of my jaw with her fingers—which at first arouses me, but then repulses me as I am overcome by the certainty that it is not my own jaw that she is touching—I am at last compelled to break our collective spell and speak.

"You told me we were acquaintances before," I say,

taking her hand in mine, mirroring it so that our fingers touch tip to tip. "That wasn't true, was it?"

Meredith rolls away, the spell broken, and stares at the ceiling, her expression clouded with emotion I can't read.

"No," she says. "It wasn't true. I wanted...I couldn't tell you."

"Okay," I say, reaching out with a consoling hand.

"What do you remember?" she says to me, turning back to look at me with her unreadable eyes. I shake my head and shrug.

"I don't know. Bits and pieces. I remember the Order. Lasinha. Some of my life here. So much of it doesn't make sense."

"It wouldn't," she says, her words escaping her like a sigh of relief. "Not until you have the whole of it. Or most of it."

"That worries you."

"It does," she says. "I have my orders. If your memory comes back, I'm supposed to bring you in. I should be doing that right now. But I can't do it."

"Why not?"

She leans over to kiss me, her mouth hungry, her tears running down my cheek. "Let's not talk about it anymore," she says. "Let's just enjoy this while we have the time."

She kisses me again and I offer no objections.

44

When I opened the door to the hotel room and saw the woman facing me, I could not disguise the shock I felt, or the growing sense of horror that curdled in my stomach once it had passed as I realized what her presence here meant.

"Not who you were expecting," she said, pushing her way past me into the room.

It was not a question and I did not answer, closing the door behind her, trying to steady my hands as I did so. I watched as she paced around the room, checking the closet and the bathroom to assure herself that we were alone. The room's sad décor seemed to disgust her, and she ran a finger along the night table and inspected it as though expecting to find dust or grime coating it.

"Everybody knows?" I said to her, unable to stand the silence any longer, wanting to get this over with.

She turned her attention to me. "There are no secrets in the Order. You should know that by now. Everybody is watching everyone. All the time."

I nodded and sat down in one of the chairs by the window. There was another across from me and she sat in it, looking vaguely uncomfortable and lost in its deep back and oversized arms. In another situation I might have laughed at the sight of this all-powerful woman subjected to the furniture of a cheap hotel, but all I could think about was that they knew. They knew about the one thing that I had tried, with painstaking effort, to keep secret. The question now was, what would they do?

The woman was watching me as I processed this, something like a smile touching her lips. It was infuriating that I could never tell what she was thinking. "He knows about you," I said, hoping the words would land like a blow. "He knows that you're conspiring against him."

"Yes," she said, unconcerned, "I'm sure you told Lasinha all that you saw and heard. Just like I'm sure all the others did before, just like the man who is following me today will."

I swallowed. The room seemed very still, the silence heavy with hushed breath. She knew then, not Lasinha and the Grand Regent. There might still be a chance to ensure that it remained so.

"What happens when I tell them about today? You've all but admitted your guilt to me. They trust me. No matter his feelings for you, he will act," I said, the certainty I felt resounding in my voice.

"The plans are in motion, even as we speak," she said, still unworried. "Where do you think he and Lasinha are? No, I have no plans on using this sordid little affair against you. I doubt I could. If I know, they will soon enough."

"Then what are you here for?"

She smiled, but there was only sadness in it. "The man who followed me here is going to want to know who I'm meeting. When he finds that out and reports it to Lasinha and Molijc, what do you think they will do?

"They will come to you," she continued, answering her own question. "They will come to you and ask you for an explanation of why you were here and who you were waiting for in this hotel room. What will you tell them?"

There was no answer to that question that did not end

in my being excommunicated, I realized. Or worse. I touched a hand to my head, worried that I was going to faint.

"They trust me. I have proven myself. I could tell them anything and they would believe it."

"They don't even trust themselves," she said, standing up. She brushed off the seat of her pants, as if the chair might have transmitted some pestilence to her. "You are faithful vessel, David Aeida. A faithful vessel. Always a vessel. That's all he sees of any of us. Vessels."

She walked toward the door and I watched her go, unable to move from my seat, to stop this disaster before it consumed me. But it was too late already, I knew, no matter what I did now. She stopped as she came to the door and turned back one last time and said, "Good luck, David Aeida. Remember to look for me."

45

Meredith is still asleep when I awake in the predawn darkness. She is so exhausted from our efforts and whatever aftereffects remain from the pulse discharge that she doesn't even stir as I slip out of the bed, disengaging my limbs from hers, and pulling on my clothes. I watch her as she slumbers, a blank, peaceful look on her face, and my warring emotions do battle again. Part of me very much wants to climb back in with her and never leave, to continue with this existence for as long as we can.

But I know that will not be for long now. I feel on the precipice of understanding. It is there within me, I am certain—not a void, but a dam that is near to bursting. When the lights return I will know for sure.

As I leave the room, I pick up Meredith's clothes and take them with me, and under the kitchen lights I go through the contents of her various pockets. Most of it is unremarkable, but for a set of what appears to be car keys. At first I set them aside, but something about the rounded plastic shell dangling from the key ring makes me pick it up again.

I expect to see buttons for automatic locks and the trunk, stamped with the little graphics that never fail to confuse me when I am trying to determine which one to press. But none of that is there. Instead, there are three round buttons with no indication of what they do, beyond a thin layer of color that encircles each of them. One green, one blue, and one red.

A communication device? An alarm of some sort? Who is to say?

I don't press any of the buttons and go to the bathroom, taking it with me. As I noticed the day before, it was renovated recently and has a drop ceiling that can be lifted away. When I finish relieving myself, I stand on the toilet and lift up the ceiling tile directly above me, resting it on the tile behind. I peer within and can make out pipes intersecting, and an inky blackness beyond where the ceiling extends past the bathroom. I take the keys and throw them as deep into the blackness as I can manage.

They disappear without a sound, and I peer around until I am certain they are beyond both sight and reach. I replace the tile above me, taking the time to make sure that it is settled and perfectly in place. My efforts have disturbed some fine white dust, which rained down below. I crouch on the floor, sweeping away all the dust from the toilet, counter, and floor, until no evidence remains.

As I duck my head around the toilet to check one last time for debris, I notice it. Carved on the wall, in a space where only someone ducking their head between the toilet and cupboards beneath the sink would see it. In lettering so tiny and precise it seems almost beyond belief, given the effort it would take to get a hand with a knife in there to etch the words. Whoever did this, hadn't been able to see what they were writing as they carved it.

It was me. There is no doubt in my mind. The words tell me as much: *Look for her.*

The sun is a glimmer on the horizon, the sky heavy with clouds that promise rain, as I pull out onto the highway, heading back into Vancouver and my apartment.

The roads are empty, given the hour, though by the time I cross the bridge and get on Kingsway I am joined by other grim-faced and solitary travelers on their way to whatever reckoning their day will bring. I drive in silence, the radio off, even my thoughts, always so teeming and contrary, seem to absent themselves. I feel both exhilaration and terror at what I am certain is to be my moment of discovery, when all of this madness will begin to make sense.

I have Meredith's phone with me and at some point on the trip I throw it out the window and watch in the mirror as it impacts with the pavement in a scatter of plastic. My own phone is still dead and I remind myself to see to that. Without her phone and whatever it was I threw into the wall—assuming it is a communication device as well—Meredith will have no method of contacting anyone. Which means she will be waiting for me at the house when I am done. I am not sure how I feel about that.

I stay on Kingsway until it merges with Main, then turn right on East Sixth Avenue and feel my hands begin to shake. I have no idea what I am looking for here, and part of me doesn't want to know. The memories that have returned to me are disquieting enough—what else remains submerged? Part of me wants to go back to Meredith, to stay with her as long as we can until oblivion seizes me again.

I have to know what has happened to me, though. I have to know.

I pass the park and turn left, spotting the couple with the German Shepherd as I go. They do not appear to give me so much as a glance, but I still go cold at the sight of them. It cannot be a simple coincidence that they are here again, I tell myself. There are no coincidences here. I pull over and park, watching them through my rearview mirror as they wander through the park, playing with their dog. After ten minutes they leave, heading away from me, and I allow myself to relax. Only when they disappear from view do I get out of the car and head for the apartment.

The building, by all appearances, is unchanged, the hallways still over-warm and stale smelling, and my apartment is as I had left it. It feels out of time as I look on it, nothing moved from when I last saw it. There is a fine layer of dust, undisturbed, on the counters and tables. A good sign, I think. No one has been here. I try not to think about how long it has been since I was here, for I have no sense.

The passage of time has moved so strangely since I became aware. All the memories that have returned to me feel distant, as though great gulf of time has passed between those events and the here and now. It is, in part, that dislocation that leads to my sense that the memories are not my own. Meredith explained it all, though I have no faith in her explanations. They scraped my mind, tamped it, protecting that precious cargo. And like that, everything from the last eight months, perhaps even longer, disappeared.

I still feel the vague tingle of the familiar pricking at my senses as I go from room to room. It feels like a place I know intimately. There is so much that seems familiar, so much that lurks just beyond my grasp. I refuse to believe that all that happened to me during those empty days is truly gone. They are the skeleton key to all my memories.

I begin in the kitchen and proceed through the living room and my bedroom, emptying every drawer, peering into every nook and cranny. All I find are paychecks and other paperwork from the life of Joseph Aurellano. The closets provide nothing as well, while the bathroom only shows the face I can't bear to look at. In despair, I return to the living room and throw myself on the couch, trying to choke back my sobs. The words of the man from my nightmare, the man I now know is the Grand Regent, return to me: *Still looking, I see.*

Still looking. The words make me sit up, awareness slowly taking hold. I fumble for my cell phone, cursing as I confirmed yet again that it is dead. The woman is the key. She has always been the key. The Grand Regent's wife. I followed her and was followed and she was witness to much of the same madness as I. She was with Osahi and helped me escape his clutches. And she conspired against me, ensuring that this would be my fate. I think of Ana, her face blank, without recognition, and feel a chill.

Why did they do it to me? I do not believe for a second the line Meredith gave me about possessing some secret knowledge that needed protection. All of my memories seem to revolve around surveillance and the Watchers' Order, which means that I likely know things others don't want found out. That they want hidden even from myself.

Why not kill me, then? But the Church doesn't look kindly on that. My relationship with Meredith is a mystery as well. Nothing in the memories I have now hints at anything between us. Is she the one I was waiting for in the hotel? No, I think, it is someone else, but I cannot remember whom.

The woman, though, will have the answers I am looking for. Somewhere, I recall, as I stare at my dead phone, I saw a charger. The desk. In a frenzy, I empty the contents of its drawers on the floor until I discover it. I plug it in and turn it on, watching the screen slowly come alight, trying to stay calm as I do so. Once it is working, I scan through my contacts, looking to see if there is a name that triggers a response. And there it is. Laila.

Meredith had even mentioned her. What had she said? "She was trouble." With the implication that we were a couple.

I press her name, opening our chat string, and begin to scroll rapidly through the texts. Two things are readily apparent: over the last eight months she sent me hundreds of texts and not once did I reply. There are no texts beyond eight months ago, so after the last time I supposedly lost my memory. This phone might be new, or maybe the Order cleaned it after their last procedure, which I presume they performed on me to restore whatever installed personality they gave me the first time.

The first time. How many times were there? The thought horrifies me, and my hands start to shake so much I have to set aside the phone.

When I manage to calm myself I return to Laila's texts, scrolling back to the top to look at the most recent messages. The last one was sent three weeks ago. Just before my latest amnesia, in all likelihood.

It reads simply: _Remember._

The word is hyperlinked, a tantalizing blue, but I resist it for the moment, scrolling further down the list. Most of the messages are short as well, a phrase or a single word only. A code of some sort that I no longer recognize.

The highlands are in bloom. Go see where the wild roses grow. There are references to threshing and tilling that I do not comprehend, though I presume them to be agricultural terms.

She used the same sort of terminology the time I followed her to the bar and listened to her conversation. At the time I thought it meant she was ready to move against the Grand Regent. Does that mean we are now involved in some conspiracy together? As I continue to scroll through the texts, hoping one of them will trigger my memory, something else catches my eye. The texts are sent one a day, or every other day, never more than one at a time, always late at night or very early in the morning.

Both of these facts seem strange to me, though I can't say exactly why. Perhaps that was when she was certain I would be alone, but the use of the code suggests she expected other eyes to view them as well. There are any number of possible explanations, but I cannot shake the feeling that I am missing something important.

Leaving that aside for the moment, I scroll back to the last message she sent, wondering what she wanted me to remember and what sparked her silence. No doubt both are connected to whatever caused my amnesia and precipitated all the events that followed. My finger hovers over the hyperlink as I am suddenly overwhelmed by trepidation. Do I even want to remember?

I press the link and the screen on my phone goes black before bursting into light.

46

The light is blue and green, edged with gold. A line of a thousand such circles, with frayed edges, going bright and dim and bright again. I shudder as it pulses into being and disappears, only to reappear at the periphery of my vision. I drop the phone and clutch my head, squeezing my eyes shut, trying to will the lights away. But they come again, emerging from deep within the depths of my vision, the dark veil I can never pierce, and burst forth, blinding me.

The device, jury-rigged from scraps I had collected over the last months, hissed and whirred as its battery warmed. Assembling it had been a painstaking, secretive effort, one that I had managed to keep hidden from Meredith and the others who watched my every waking moment, for signs that I had emerged from the slumber they had placed me in. Even now it was hard to keep straight who I was, the swirl of various memories all colliding, metamorphosing into strange hybrids. Every moment felt as though I had two thoughts, two perspectives informing me. My hands trembled as I reached out to start the channeling, a side effect of the procedures the Acolytes had performed on me.

Meredith suspected, I thought, she suspected. She knew me too well for me to be able to hide from her as I did even from myself. She would catch me looking at her in a way I never did, or I would say something, a phrase, a tone of voice, the smallest of things, and she would look at me and know. I could not help revealing myself, just as she could not help allowing me to surface for those tantalizing moments, our desires at war with our good sense and duty. No more, though.

My head feels like it is on fire. Every neuron seems to be firing at the same instant, an explosion of thought and emotion beyond my comprehension. It is too much at once, I can only clutch my head and beg for it to end. I lie on the floor for what feels like hours, awash in sensation, though I know it is only a few minutes, each one of them agonizing beyond belief.

At last the current coursing through me ebbs and I am able to open my eyes and raise myself up to my knees. I am lost again, not recognizing anything.

It's your apartment.

I blink and the room comes into focus, a sort of equilibrium returning to me. As it does, the woman—Laila—stands up from the couch and approaches me. I look at her in a daze: how did she get here? I open my mouth to speak, but my tongue is paralyzed. She gives me a reassuring look and gestures for me to follow her.

The blue indicators blinked in a strange pattern that slowly approached synchronicity, indicating that the channels were nearing alignment. Once that happened I would be able to cross over. I tried not to think about what would happen on the other side, of those waiting for me, and the work to be done. One step at a time.

The room was quiet but for the device, almost ominously so when factoring in the gloom that shrouded the empty space. It was an empty office space above a coffee shop, the Cafe Beano, long unrented, which I had borrowed for my purposes. There was a bank of windows looking over Broadway below, but the ancient, dust-covered blinds were drawn tight. The door was at the far end of the room and I kept glancing toward it, though I knew it was locked and secure. I also knew that would do little to stop those pursuing me.

The seconds ticked by, each one more anxious then the last, as the lights refused to synchronize, the pattern still incoherent. Every moment was one I could not spare, for I knew with a sickening certainty that the Order monitor was closing in on me. And I could only wait. And hope.

The indicators began to blink more rapidly, approaching unison, the moment here. The air around the device began to change, the molecules seized by a strange current, and began to ripple. It was almost visible to the eye, and soon I could almost make out the room in the other world, a similar room, in a similar building, in a similar place. It was hazy, not quite there. I could hear a voice, distant and marred by a kind of static, saying, "Another five seconds."

I did not hear the door open, but I felt the presence of someone in the room and whirled around to see Meredith standing there, a grim expression on her face.

"You're too late," I said, as the telltale chime sounded, echoed on the other side by its mate.

"I don't think so," Meredith said, and jangled her car keys in front of me.

It confused me for a moment, and that was enough to freeze me where I stood. Too late I realized they were not car keys, but the suppressant. The button glowed green in the shadows and I watched, sick with horror and fury, unable to do anything, as she pressed the button and my thoughts dissolved into darkness.

In the last moments of awareness that were left to me I watched as someone crossed over from the other world. I looked at her blankly, already no longer able to recall her name. The woman looked from me to Meredith. "What is—"

She did not have a chance to finish, a knife flashing in Meredith's hand plunging into her throat. Seizing this final opportunity, I stumbled to my feet and leapt into the channel, knowing nothing more than that it was essential that I cross over. It was difficult to move, difficult even to remember how to put each foot in front of the other. Ahead of me was the other room, a wavering place, brightening and then dimming. I could hear Meredith give a belated cry behind me as she noticed my progress, but it was a distant thing. The voices on the other side were nearer, warmer sounding, and I moved toward them.

A shout on the other side alerted me to the fact that something was wrong. The other room began to dissolve, vanishing as I took another step, leaving me in this vacant office. I turned around to see the ruins of a strange device and a woman crouched over it, a knife in her hand. Another woman lay on the floor, blood pooling underneath her. I ran from the room, ignoring the woman's cries, going down the stairs and outside into the blinding sunlight.

Laila takes me to the bathroom, gesturing for me to look under the sink. I duck my head below, expecting to find another message carved into the wall, but it is empty. I look at it blankly and glance back up at the woman, expecting to find further guidance, but she is gone. The tiles on the floor have flowerlike patterns that appear to form eyes at each corner. I imagine them watching me, wondering if I am losing my mind.

The woman is back a moment later, crouching beside me, motioning with her hand toward the tiles where the floor joins the wall. I reach out and run my hand along the floor, and my fingertips find the edges where one of the tiles has been cut. I pry it up and discover the floor underneath has been hollowed out. Within the crevice there is a plastic bag with a phone and a charger within. Not even looking to see if the woman is following me, I go to living room and plug the phone in and turn it on.

There are no contacts in the phone, and when I go to the log I see that only one number has ever been called. My own. I blink furiously and my hands begin to shake again. I go to the text messages and there they are. Every message Laila sent to me is there. I whirl around, expecting to see the woman again, ready to guide me further. She is gone, the apartment feels empty, is empty but for me.

I am Laila. I am the voice.

"I am David Aeida," I say aloud, staring at my hands. This is my body, these are my hands.

I am not.

47

Before I leave the apartment I return the cell phone to the crevice, adding the transponder I stole from the Seeker, which I seal in its own baggie, and carefully cover over with the tile. That done, I go to the Cafe Beano and have a sandwich and an Americano and begin to feel more myself. When I am finished with the sandwich, I slip upstairs into the vacant office, using my old methods. Tradecraft, is the word. Is it my skill or David Aeida's that I am putting to use? Or are they now one and the same?

As I suspected, the room is empty. Nothing remains of all my careful and exacting work, all those moments in days and nights when I took Aeida unawares, guiding him without his even realizing it. Whispers and thoughts unbidden. A monumental effort ruined in an instant. The body is gone as well, no sign of any blood. Yasmin was her name.

Pushing those thoughts from my mind, I return to the apartment for the keys to Aeida's car. It still seems incredible to me that the Order left me with a means of escape from Meredith's watchful eye. But then, why wouldn't they? She proved herself more than capable. The keys and car are still there; no one had the chance to remove them in case things went even further sideways then they had already. The Seeker's arrival would have everyone scrambling. Things would be missed. I can only hope that will aid me in the days to come.

I return to Kingsway, heading back to the farmhouse. There is no point to it, I know. Even some danger, in the unlikely event Meredith recovered the suppressant. What is left to say? Everything.

Nightfall approaches, the sun lazy in its descent from the sky behind me, as I turn off the highway and back onto the gravel roads that lead to the farmhouse. My head aches from all I have undergone, and I can feel the steady pull of exhaustion wearing at me, my eyes narrow and heavy as they peer into the distance. I fight against the embrace of sleep, of letting go and forgetting all this. Soon enough it will be over.

To occupy my mind, I turn to cataloging my memories. There are still some gaps here and there, minor things I think for the most part. The void is gone and these are but blank spaces, indrawn breaths awaiting an exhalation, and I feel confident they will soon be filled. The Aeida memories are all still there, though they only go so far back. The first thing I can really remember with any clarity is my first meeting with Lasinha in front of the Vancouver Public Library. I know, in a general sense, the shape of my life before that, where I lived, what I did, but I have no specific memories associated with it.

Strange. Perhaps there was not room for both of us in here. The thought makes me laugh aloud, but I stop abruptly, disturbed by the sound. Was there a tinge of madness to it?

I had not known exactly what the Grand Regent's plan was when I intercepted myself on my sordid rendezvous in the hotel, only that it would involve a personality transplant of some manner. Mine into his. His into mine. That was my thought. I never imagined the Acolytes were more skilled than that. After my visit I knew the Grand Regent would choose him as the vessel, and my desperate hope was that the triggers I placed within his mind would set him on the trail to finding me. And, in a sense, they had. I am found, though I have no idea where my body is or who is in possession of it.

Meredith, though, will have the answers I need.

She is waiting for me when I pull up behind the house, leaning against the doorway on the back porch. As I get out of the car I see a cascade of emotion dance across her face, vanishing as I approach her, the mask returning to its place. I stop in front of her and she stands up straight, crossing her arms across her chest.

"Found yourself, did you?"

"Yes," I say. "And now I have some questions."

"Why don't we go in, have something to eat?" she says, gesturing with her head into the house. All the lights are off, except for the kitchen, its dim glow just reaching the doorway.

"I won't be long."

Meredith nods, fighting her emotions again. "I'm sorry."

"A little late for that." She seems about to say something in reply, but manages to stop herself. "What did he do to me?" I say.

Meredith smiles faintly, looking past me and into the gathering shadows. "A personality transplant."

"It was more than that. Aeida is still here."

"That was the plan. A double tamp. You and then him. They tamped him, scraped him, put in a few other safety mechanisms in case another Acolyte went digging in there. The plan was he would never know it was there, especially not in his scraped state. Molijc wanted to make sure no one would find you."

"Why not just kill me?" I say, surprising myself at the desolation in my voice.

"I begged him to. But he said he needed you. Needed your body anyway. The wife of the Grand Regent cannot just disappear without a few questions being asked. And he couldn't leave you in there. There was always the chance you would come back."

A flock of birds takes flight, cawing and wheeling about the sky, incandescent with color in these last moments of the day. We watch them for a moment, hushed amidst their cacophony.

"He wanted me to suffer," I say, breaking our silence, and she nods. "But it didn't work."

"No," she says, her voice suddenly very small. "The Acolytes didn't understand. Maybe the tamps were never stable. Maybe it just wasn't possible for it to be stable. You kept coming back."

I take a step away from her, overwhelmed by déjà vu and horror.

"How many times?" I say to her as she stares at the ground, refusing to meet my eyes. "How many times? We've had this conversation before, haven't we?"

Still she will not look at me, staring off into the gathering night. My hands are shaking and I take another step away from her. Is there an extraction squad out there, waiting for her signal? No, I took her cell phone. I took the suppressant. There is no phone line here, no means for her to contact anyone.

"Well, this is the last time," I say at last, my voice breaking with emotion.

She looks back at me, her eyes unreadable.

"I can't believe you used me like this," I say, looking past her and into the house, remembering those idyllic hours in this Eden, now poisoned forever by knowledge.

My words shake her and she responds with venom, her eyes volcanic with fury. "That takes some nerve, even for you," she says. "You two passed me around like your plaything. Using me to get to the other. I loved you. I loved you."

It is difficult to breathe; tears sting my eyes. "I loved you too. And you paid me back by betraying me to him. But you've had your revenge now, haven't you? You've gotten to play with me. How many times was I back just enough that you could seduce me? Was that your end of the bargain?"

"Bargain?" she says, incredulous. "You think this is a bargain. That I want to be here. I'm here because he doesn't trust me anymore. This is my punishment. To watch over you. To watch you come back and hate me and then to make you disappear again."

She sobs, her whole body shaking with each breath. I want, more than anything, to go to her, to take her into my arms and cry with her, tell her that I understand, that we both have suffered too much at his hands. So many have suffered. But not this time. I will not go to her again. I turn away and start to walk to the car. She looks up at me, disbelieving, reaching out with one hand as though to draw me to her.

"Goodbye, Meredith," I say, getting into the car.

As I do she falls to the ground, imploring me to come to her, begging for forgiveness. "I won't betray you. Please. I won't."

I turn the car on, driving out and back onto the road, not looking back once. I do not dare. The desolation in her eyes was almost too much to bear. I head off into the growing darkness, wanting to be gone.

EXCERPT:

THE APOSTATE
VOLUME TWO OF THE SOJOURNERS
CYCLE

With her self restored but not her body, Laila has only one goal in mind. To have her revenge upon the Grand Regent for all he has done to her. First, though, she needs to find her way home across the universes.

That is easier said than done. The Grand Regent's agents in the Watchers' Order are still pursuing her. As is the Society of Travellers. And the Seeker lurks somewhere, waiting for his moment to strike.

Laila has a plan, though, and a few tricks of her own. But she will soon discover that not everything is at seems and there is no one she can trust.

1

The days drift, one into another, aimless and wandering as I am. The realization of my true identity, composite and shifting as it is, paralyzes me. After so long seeing myself as David Aeida, trying to stay free and survive long enough to regain my memory and myself, to face this new person, complete and whole, is almost too much. It is all there, all that I have done and all that has been done to me. There is no escaping it.

I tell myself I have the luxury of time, as I work to avoid facing the consequences of what has happened. The Travelers will not allow the Seeker to return to this world, at least not immediately. They will be more concerned with the damage that might be incurred by his return than whatever harm I might be able to manage. As far as they know, I am a native of this place.

And I am going nowhere; that much they know as well. They might send others to investigate. There is Osahi's extraction squad and the Watchers' Compound to be dealt with. But I feel confident I can avoid their grasp. I have done so before, in other times and other places.

Meredith, and whichever other of Molijc's foot soldiers are in this universe, presents a far more pressing concern.

How long, I wonder, will it take for her to escape the farmhouse and find some method of communication to the Watchers? There are not many with her, I believe. There was no one but her in the compound. The man who drove us to the compound was, I now recall, one of Aeida's fellow Regents from this world. There is Williams, whose apartment we used that first day. Who else?

I struggle with this thought until I realize it is of no consequence. I can avoid them as easily as I avoid the Travelers. They will need numbers, an extraction team, to find me, and they cannot hope to get them across now. Not after I escaped the Seeker. The Travelers will seal the universe, and they will be watching sub-signals for any channels that someone might try to open. Even communication across the universes will be difficult. Meredith will need the equipment in Lasinha's compound in order to manage it, and she dares not return there.

So I am safe for the moment, though I know that is illusory. I am not safe at all; I am trapped, and everyone—the Seeker and the Travelers, Meredith and the Watchers, and Molijc himself—can all afford to wait for circumstances to change, knowing that I will be here. It is clear I have to find some means of escaping this universe into another, if I am to have any hope of regaining my body and my life from the man who stole it from me. But doing so seems utterly hopeless. Not only do I face the impossible task of crossing from this universe, while avoiding the Travelers' notice, once I manage that feat I have to then find what the Grand Regent has done with my body and find an Acolyte who can extract me from Aeida and return me to my proper place.

It is all too much to think of, so instead I wallow in memory, chasing my thoughts down too-familiar byways. They all lead inescapably to despair. What a fate Molijc engineered for me. It is not torture enough to disappear me from the Church, put me in another's body in a forgotten universe—he made certain that Meredith would be there when I returned. He knows enough of the Acolytes' imperfect art to know that I would eventually emerge from whatever vessel he placed me in. And as I was born again each time, he wanted me to be faced with Meredith, knowing that neither of us would be able resist falling into familiar patterns.

Only I broke free this time, I defied him. I tore myself from the trap, leaving whatever limb remained behind, cauterizing the wound and going away. To where? Nowhere. I wander the city, going from place to place, staying nowhere long, refusing to do what I know must be done.

I have dreams of abandoning the faith, the center of my life for so many years, and finding my way in this new universe. If I could manage to squirrel myself away somewhere, the Society and the Order might lose interest eventually. Events would lead them elsewhere, would they not? And I could find peace away from this madness I am embroiled in. So much of it is of my own creation that I cannot even feel sorry for myself.

It is utter fantasy; I know that. Deep in these false bones, I know that. Aeida knows that too. We both understand Molijc all too well. Now that I have slipped free of his prison, he will not stop until he has me in his grasp again. He is beyond all reason, a monster. As is the Society. The Travelers' lust for power knows no bounds, and they will want to make an example of anyone like me who has defied them.

Am I any better than they? It is a hard question, and I fear the answer.

All I know is that the true faith has been central to my life for so long that I know nothing else. De Gofroy guided me. I sat at his feet and he taught me so much about myself and the universes. He told me I would be instrumental in finding the one true universe and in guiding the faith to its destiny. Part of me believes it still, no matter all that has transpired in the years since.

There is so much doubt in me now, where there was none before. How many have suffered as I have—or worse, perished—as a result of what Molijc and Lasinha have done in the name of the faith? And I cannot forget the extraction squad, killed by my hand, because in my vanity I believe I am central to the survival of the Church and the continuance of the true faith.

I am as mad as Molijc, and it is only my failure to topple him that has spared others from suffering the wounds I might inflict. What is this faith worth if all it leads to is destruction? Where is the light De Gofroy promised? Around me I see only darkness.

2

The only memories of my own that remain unclear, shrouded somewhat by the mists of Acolyte procedures, are of the last months—or years, perhaps, though I refuse to believe this nightmare has gone on that long—when I emerged from my slumber within the Aeida vessel. It is impossible for me to separate one instance from another, for they seem always to be the same. Inevitably I am drawn to the farmhouse outside Mission, my dimly remembered past taking me there, where I find myself acting out a charade of those half-memories with Meredith until the Acolytes do their work again.

Does he make her report all of it to him? He would and she would, in the desperate, impossible hope that he will forgive her and allow her to return to his graces. He is a madman. But she knows that and does not care. For a very long time, I did not either.

It is the thought of her reporting to him again about my escape, imagining his incandescent rage, that at last sparks the desire in me to act. I must escape. I cannot go back to the way things were. My only hope lies in leaving this universe. No matter how difficult it might be, I have to find a way. Two lives are at stake: mine and Aeida's.

He remains within me as well—what is left of him, anyway. His more recent memories, beginning from the time he joined the Church of the Regents, are there and mostly intact, or so it feels to me. Anything before that time is filled with gaps, half formed and cast in darkness. I can recall what his mother looked like, can feel the touch of her hand upon my shoulder, but her voice has disappeared. Her mouth moves, forming words, and I know what they are, but she does not speak. Her touch, so distant and so rare, still fills me with the strange amalgam of dread and need that sent me on this endless search for the shape of some meaning that might replace it all.

It is strange to think Aeida's thoughts as though they are my own, though I find myself doing it at moments when my guard is down. I will have to watch that. He is not a silent member of this partnership, as much as I want him to be. His knowledge of this Vancouver, a city I am only passingly familiar with in my own universe, is invaluable to me. It will be instrumental in what I must do, and on that we can both agree. It must be done.

I sidle up to my objective, circling toward it over the period of a day. Caution must always be my watchword, for it is only a matter of time before I am discovered. I must work to ensure that I give myself as much time as I can before the inevitable happens. Only when I am absolutely certain I am not being followed or observed do I at last approach the university campus on the peninsula's edge.

There is an old grey-stoned library there, towering and gothic, seemingly the repository of arcane and mysterious knowledge. I know that what lies within there is but a shadow of the truth, for no one here understands the true nature, the multiplicity of the universe and of existence. The library is largely empty, as is the campus, it still being several weeks before September and the start of term. I pass through the main entrance and into the narrow stacks, the stench of aged and damp parchment heavy in the air, and go below down a thin stairway. The lower levels are crowded with shelves, low-ceilinged and windowless, with a hint of mildew to the air.

The shelves are crammed with books of all sizes and shape, giving everything an appearance of disorder, even as there are signs posted at each row showing the call numbers stacked there. The numbers and letters mean nothing to me, it is like a foreign language, but I do not need them to guide me. I know where I am going. I head unerringly to the historical botany section, filled with monographs on Humboldt, Cuvier and their ilk. Crouching down, I run my hand along the bottom shelf until I find the books I am looking for, the many volumes of Humboldt's *Voyages in the New World* in the original French. None of them look as though they have been disturbed in a long while.

I count along to the fifth volume and pull it from the shelf. I have to brace myself to drag it free from what feels like a magnetic pull. With it in hand, I stand and flip it open to page 126, and am met by a wall of impenetrable text. Not seeing what I am looking for, I advance forward in the book, going by increments of three until I find the card slipped in between pages 194 and 195. Before looking at the card, I do the math: twenty-three days since I last replied. Twenty-three days since my attempt to cross over. It seems both too long and too short a time to have elapsed.

I am awash in the hum of vertigo, my legs trembling, and have to blink it away in order to focus on the card. The texture of it is very strange, feeling almost like cloth, though it is as stiff as regular paper would be. Drawn upon it is a sequence of three images: a seed just begun to sprout, a starling perched on a branch, and a table. I let out a steadying breath—all is not lost yet—and make my way, book and card in hand, to the center of the floor, where there are tables and chairs available. I borrow a pen from one of the students and sit down, studying the images again while considering my response.

My first image is a starling in flight, a signal that I am myself and ready to come across. The second image I draw is of a table that has been overturned, representing the transfer device I built in secret, and which Meredith destroyed. The third is a box with eyes upon it, which should indicate, I hope, the emergency transponder I stole from the Seeker. This is the means to get me across, if we can manage the channels without the Travelers becoming aware. Given that it is an emergency device, no doubt with beacon activation, that could prove difficult. I briefly consider adding a fourth image—another pair of eyes to indicate the universe is being watched—but they should know that already. We have people in the Society who will let us know such things.

When I am satisfied with my work, I return the card between the pages I found it and return the book to the shelf. Again I can feel the drag of something as I slip the volume into place. I linger for a moment after, though I know I should not, in case I have somehow been followed. I am confident I was not; no one has managed to find my trail yet, for I have been careful to move about the city randomly and without apparent purpose. But Meredith might know about the message drops in the library and set somebody to watch. I cannot discount the possibility, though no one is paying me any particular mind as I go about my business.

Tomorrow, when I return, will be the true test, or at the least the beginning of one. For now I will have to follow a pattern, returning here to send and receive messages, and no matter how I try to disguise it, the pattern will be there for someone to see—if they are watching, and in the Church of the Regents, someone always is.

THE APOSTATE will be available in April 2017.

ABOUT THE AUTHOR

Clint Westgard is the author of The Shadow Men Trilogy and the science fiction epic The Sojourners Cycle. In addition, he has published a work of historical fantasy set in colonial Peru, The Maleficio Chronicles, and a retelling of the Minotaur legend, The Trials of the Minotaur. Clint Westgard lives in Calgary, Alberta.

ALSO BY CLINT WESTGARD

The Apostate
Volume Two of The Sojourners Cycle

Laila has only one goal in mind. To have her revenge upon the Grand Regent for all he has done to her. First, though, she needs to find her way across the universes.

That is easier said than done. The Grand Regent's agents are still pursuing her. As is the Society of Travellers. And the Seeker lurks somewhere, waiting for his moment to strike.

Laila has a plan, though, and a few tricks of her own. But she will discover that not everything is at seems. For the war she has given her life to hides a far greater conflict.

Spanning multiple universes and the complexities of the human mind, The Apostate, continues the incredible journey begun in The Forgotten. The second volume of The Sojourners Cycle is an unforgettable science fiction epic that encompasses the fates of universes and humanity itself.

ALSO BY CLINT WESTGARD

The Acolyte
Volume Three of The Sojourners Cycle

After crossing the universes to join with Toma Osahi's group of renegades in their battle for control of the Church of Regents, Laila finds herself in a precarious position. While they both share the same goal—the destruction of the Grand Regent—Osahi doesn't know who Laila really is. What will he do if he finds out?

While Laila struggles to keep her identity secret, Osahi and his people pull her deeper and deeper into a search for Ana that promises to shed light on the dark secrets of the Watchers' Order and the Acolytes. Before she can find those answers though, Laila will have to face what lies within.

Crossing the universes has unsettled the already shaky equilibrium in her mind. If she wants to return herself to her own body, she will have to act fast, for the consequences of what Acolytes did to her are still reverberating. And Aeida hides somewhere, waiting for his time to come.

The thrilling third volume of the Sojourners Cycle continues Laila's incredible journey across the universes against incredible odds, as well as exploring her past, including the pivotal role she played in the rise of the Grand Regent and her own downfall at his hands.

ALSO BY CLINT WESTGARD

The Double
Volume Four of The Sojourners Cycle

David Aeida now commands his body, having cast Laila
aside. He has sworn fealty to the Grand Regent, who
wants him by his side and sees that his loyalty is rewarded.

But the Grand Regent is not the man he was. He is
paranoid and suspicious of everyone, isolated in his tower,
and thirsting for vengeance against those he feels have
wronged him. How long until he turns on Aeida as well?

That is only the beginning of Aeida's problems. For he
knows the Seeker and the Society of Travelers remain to
play their parts. Both desire nothing more than the utter
destruction of the Church of Regents and all its works.
And though Laila has been defeated, he knows better than
anyone not to assume she has been vanquished.

The epic fourth volume of the Sojourners Cycle centers
upon the many betrayals and lies at the heart of the faith of
the Church of Regents and the devastation upon the lives
of the faithful they have wrought. Desire and guilt, love
and revenge, rage and despair will drive them all, with
consequences for all the universes.

ALSO BY CLINT WESTGARD

The Sojourner
Volume Five of The Sojourners Cycle

Laila's strange and reluctant alliance with the Seeker
continues, though she does not know where it will lead
her. She fears it will place her in another prison, worse
than the one she has just managed to escape.

But her escape is not entirely complete. For though she
has been restored to her own flesh, parts of Aeida
somehow still remain. Along with some other she does not
recognize. Is this some aftereffect of the Acolyte's bizarre
procedure? Or the result of the Seeker's meddling?

All this pales in comparison to what Laila soon discovers.
That she has an unwanted part to play in an ancient
struggle for who will rule the crossings between the
universes and all that lies in them.

In the stunning conclusion to the Sojourners Cycle Laila
will be faced with a terrible choice, one that will decide her
fate and humanity's.

ALSO BY CLINT WESTGARD

Realm of Shadows
Volume One of The Shadow Men

Craitol and Renuih, two empires a world apart, divided by
the desert that lies between them. A desert ruled by the
Shadow Men.

An uneasy peace holds sway in both realms, hiding
longstanding feuds and bitter rivalries. Until a Shadow
Men raid on Renuih shatters the calm and sets in motion
events no one can control.

Masiph id Ezern, unfavored son of the Imperial Vazeir,
finds himself a hero following the raid. His father remains
unmoved by his exploits and, in his bitterness, Masiph will
find himself a reluctant participant in a plot against the
empire.

As he finds himself drawn deeper and deeper into the
conspiracy, he soon realizes there will be no escaping the
realm of shadows, where intrigue and betrayal abound.
And though the Shadow Men have gone quiet, they will
not stay silent forever…

ALSO BY CLINT WESTGARD

Council of Shadows
Volume Two of The Shadow Men

Discontent continues to fester within the realms of Craitol and Renuih, fed by intrigues carried out in the shadows. As rivals and apostates struggle for supremacy, a long incubated plan begins to unfold.

Vyissan, a mysterious alkemycal practitioner arrives in Renuih, the latest strike in a long war over who shall control the secrets of alkemya and Craitol itself. He carries with him a secret that, once revealed, will reverberate across all realms. Before he can reveal it though, the conspirators against the emperor will strike their own blow.

But now, a new and more powerful menace looms on the horizon. The Shadow Men have gained the secrets of the Council Adept's alkemya and no one can be certain what they will do with it...

ALSO BY CLINT WESTGARD

Dance of Shadows
Volume Three of The Shadow Men

War with the Shadow Men looms in both realms as the consequences of the Gvers' Council in Craitol begin to make themselves known. A war that could end in glorious triumph or bitter disaster.

Doubt shadows everyone's steps, for they know there are no certainties in the desert. Especially now the Shadow Men have made the art of alkemya their own.

No one has more questions than Vyissan, for he is working in service to a cause he is no longer sure he believes in. And now he must undertake a journey with those who both loathe and fear him. Before the first sword is drawn, his life will be under threat.

But his will not be the only one, for somewhere in the desert the Shadow Men lie in wait...

ALSO BY CLINT WESTGARD

The Maleficio Chronicles

Luisa is always more than she appears. Rumor and mystery surround her. And strange events seem to follow wherever she goes.

Born in Lima, City of Kings, to a noble family, her father so fears her true nature that he banishes her to a convent. There she falls under the suspicion of the Inquisition and decides to flee.

Disguised as a man, she embarks upon a series of wild adventures, dueling, carousing, and gambling her way across colonial Peru. But everything changes when someone recognizes her for what she truly is, and soon she finds herself fighting for her very survival.

In a world where she will always stand apart, Luisa undergoes a strange journey, marked by betrayal and murder, terrible powers and mysterious strangers. *The Maleficio Chronicles* is her incredible confession and a story like no other.

ALSO BY CLINT WESTGARD

The Devious Kind

A Mystery

The body of a local woman is found in a coulee on a ranch north of Loverna, her head blown off with a shotgun. New to town and the job, Constable Martin Thomas arrives on the scene as a spring snowstorm begins to wipe out all evidence before his investigation has even begun.

There is no shortage of suspects to consider. A spurned husband. A jealous lover. A betrayed business partner. And family members battling over an inheritance. All have motive and opportunity. And no one seems to be telling him everything.

As he tries to sift the truth from the lies, the snowstorm continues to build, leaving Loverna cut off from the outside world. And Thomas alone to face a killer who will do anything not to get caught.